Death Co Greenway

A Kate Lambert

Devon Mystery

Frances Powell

Other novels by Frances Powell

The Bodyguard
Mystery of White Horse Lake: An Irish Mystery
Ghost of Tara: An Irish Mystery

A Ballysea Mystery Series:

The O'Brien
A Bad Wind Blowing
The O'Brien: The Untold Story
A Ballysea Christmas
Matrimony is Murder

Chief Inspector Cam Fergus Mysteries

Lady of the Wye
Murder in the Royal Forest of Dean
She Lies Beneath
River Wye Dead & Breakfast

Cover by: Kim Wilson of Kiwi Cover Design

Copyright 2022

ISBN: 978-1-66786-188-3

Chapter 1

It was personal. Walking away from her career after 20 years and moving somewhere no one knew Kate was personal. Everything she did was personal.

Bathed in sweat from the same nightmare that haunted her dreams these last six months, Katherine Lambert rolled over, switched on the bedside lamp, and peered at the clock before reaching for the small-framed photograph on her nightstand. After a few minutes staring at the image there, she wiped away a tear. Today was the day she would finally do what she needed to do.

Climbing out of bed at 3 am, she pulled the damp nightgown over her head and let it drop to the floor before reaching for her robe and padding into the kitchen to put the kettle on. Five minutes later, she sat cross-legged at the small drop table that served as the only dining option in her tiny central London flat, sipping her first cup of Earl Grey. The little flat had been the perfect choice when she bought it nearly twenty years ago. She was now close enough to work that she could walk. She no longer had to deal with the train, the crowded underground, and the multiple changes needed when she lived in her childhood home. Besides the commute, living with her parents had been good for both parties. Katherine only needed to concentrate on her rising career while her mum and dad cared for her daily needs. Something that they took great pleasure in for their only child. Clean clothes seemed to find their way into Katherine's closet magically, and hot meals were always waiting for her. As her parents grew older, Katherine seamlessly took on the tasks around the house that became too difficult for them. Chief among her duties was caring for the garden and her mum's prize-winning roses. It wasn't until both her parents suddenly passed away within months of each other that Katherine left the nest. She was shocked when she found a bank statement in her parents and her name for every penny Katherine had paid them for room and board since she started working. She had vowed to manage her earnings like her parents had and save this money for her eventual retirement.

Her new neighborhood was resplendent with restaurants and takeaways for those evenings after a long shift when she couldn't face cooking. Returning to her flat on Friday evenings with her regular fish n chips from the local corner chippie made Katherine miss her mum's healthy and delicious dinners. A small smile flittered across Katherine's face when she recalled the first day she viewed the flat and noticed the little rear garden, a feature of these ground-floor flats. A single rose bush that a previous owner had planted, then left to its own resources, cried out for help from Katherine's green fingers. It was that single, struggling rose bush that sealed the deal. Prices in this area of London had skyrocketed, and the smallest of flats were commanding high prices. Small as it was, it had been an excellent investment.

After a long steamy shower, Katherine carefully dressed for the day. Today was going to mark a change in every aspect of Katherine's life. She had slid the envelope under her boss's door after leaving work and knew that the compulsory meeting with her boss and mentor would happen as soon as she reported to work first thing in the morning. It was not a meeting that she was looking forward to for once in her career.

Katherine grabbed a cup of coffee on the way into the office from the café next door and hurried into the imposing grey building that had been her place of employment for the last twenty years. She needed all the strength she could garnish to face her boss. Climbing the two flights of stairs that lead to her section, Katherine went over and over in her mind how she would answer the inevitable questions. Chief among them, why was she throwing away her career?

Pushing open the door, her colleagues stopped what they were working on and stared silently at her. She hadn't even reached her desk when Commander Morgan's door flew open, "In my office now, Lambert."

Dropping her purse and coffee off at her desk, she started towards the office door, then turned and returned for her coffee. "I think I'll need this," she said aloud, causing some colleagues to chuckle. They were aware that the boss was in a snit but had no idea the gravity of the situation. Katherine was well-liked and respected by her male and female subordinates, rare in the police force.

Closing the door behind her, Katherine stood facing the man who had mentored her over the last twenty years.

"Sit down and tell me what the meaning of this letter is," he said, shaking the letter in his hand.

Not one to mince words, Katherine replied, "It's my letter of resignation from the Force, Sir."

"I'm not illiterate, Lambert. I can read. You know very well what I mean. I know the last six months have been difficult for you, and I sympathize. It's never easy to lose a colleague. Believe me; I have been in your same position more times than I care to remember."

"I very much doubt that, Sir. I don't think your wife would have tolerated it."

Sitting back in his chair, it finally dawned on Morgan what Katherine was alluding to, "Are you telling me that you and Sanders were in a relationship, Katherine?" his tone softening.

"Yes, Sir, Dan and I were engaged to be married. Today would have been our wedding day."

Rising from his desk, Morgan turned his back and stared out the window, "So, no one else knew about your relationship?"

"No, Sir, we were very discreet. No one in the office had any idea. We were both the only child of our parents, and with both sets of parents dead, there was no family to tell. That makes you the first and only person I have told, except the registrar at the license bureau."

Sitting back down and reaching across his desk, he placed his large hand over her small cold hand before saying, "I am so sorry for your loss. I understand now what has caused the change in you these past six months. I wish you'd told me sooner and not in this way. I can completely understand your decision to resign, but I'm afraid I can't accept this based on what you just told me. I have to give you compulsory bereavement leave, and you'll have to speak to a counselor before the higher-ups allow you to take early retirement. What I am going to suggest is six months' leave, and at the end of that time, if you still want to resign, I'll submit your paperwork. You'll be on full pay and benefits during that time. Does that sound fair?"

"Six months won't make a difference in my choice, but I agree," replied Katherine as she stood to leave.

Standing to face her and extending his hand, Morgan asked, "What shall I tell your colleagues?"

"My flat is on the market, so perhaps just that I'm in the middle of moving. That won't be a lie. I'll work out the rest of this week, and then you can tell the team."

"How do you plan to make a living in your retirement? If you don't mind me asking?"

"I've always loved writing, and I think with my background, I might be able to make a career from it," replied Katherine.

Solemnly nodding, Morgan replied, "It has been my extreme pleasure to watch you rise through the ranks and be your commanding officer. I hope you will change your mind and return to us, but if not, I wish you the very best."

Chapter 2

As the 4:50 train from Paddington Station sped through the dark English Countryside, the passing train's blaring whistles and noise woke her from her nap, and peering out the window, the elderly lady saw a woman being strangled on the opposite train. Witnessing a murder in a train running parallel to yours would certainly seem unusual to most people, but not Agatha Christie. She wove her mysteries around everyday events like taking a train from London.

Katherine Lambert had left behind life in London to do as Agatha had done those many years ago. She would have her English Riviera summer in one short weekend at Agatha Christy's Greenway before looking for a permanent home in the area. Leaving London's Paddington Station, Katherine curled up in her first-class seat with her well-worn favorite Christie mystery, the *4:50 from Paddington,* and quickly passed the 3-hour journey to Paignton. From there, she boarded the Dartmouth Steam Railway's train to Greenway Halt.

Before pulling up to the rural platform, Katherine slipped into her trusty walking boots, threw her backpack over her shoulder, and prepared for the 30-minute woodland walk bringing her to Greenway. She was glad that she'd done some research because, as forewarned, the shade from the canopy of trees had indeed left the path muddy and slippery in places, and she was thankful for the extra grip and protection from the elements that her boots provided.

Katherine's first sighting of the 1780s clotted cream-hued Georgian house, beautifully perched on manicured lawns sloping down to the River Dart, made her understand in a second why the author had chosen this

7

home for her summer retreat. Surrounded on three sides by water and backed by beautiful woodlands and even more glorious gardens, it was the ideal place to unwind and refuel. It would be the perfect place to de-stress from the twenty-year career with the MET, of which the last ten were dealing with homicides. Maybe, she would even get some inspiration from the surroundings that would help her finally finish her first murder mystery.

Katherine had booked the weekend in the Lodge at Greenway, a charming small single-storied stone cottage in the woodland at the entrance to Greenway. After dropping off her bag at the Lodge, she was off to walk the gardens and view some places on the estate her idol had used in her mysteries.

Walking around the gardens, Katherine quickly found her way to the Boathouse. This beautiful boathouse that had now sadly fallen into disrepair was the crime scene in 'Dead Man's Folly.' The once highly ornate interior, which offered stunning views across the river and a peaceful retreat, now suffered from the elements that make its location so idyllic. As one of the many helpful volunteer guides explained, the lower plunge pool allowed the saltwater in from the River Dart at high tide, permitting the residents of Greenway to take the waters. She wondered if Agatha had herself taken the plunge. Katherine was relieved to hear that a lengthy restoration project was underway by the National Trust, paid for by funds raised from the sale of raffle tickets and through the work of generous volunteers to repair the effects of time. She stayed there for quite a long time, just taking in the atmosphere and the spectacular views. Looking at the lovely ornate fireplace, she imagined herself lounging in an overstuffed chair in front of a crackling fire and staring out at the water on a chilly Autumn evening as she plotted murderous scenes for her next mystery.

Mentally, Katherine noted that this would be a perfect setting for a lover's tryst ending in a crime of passion or maybe just a premeditated murder made to give that impression. Perhaps the house's cruel and cheating owner sets the scene and invites his wealthy, unsuspecting wife there to watch the sunset and drink Champaign in celebration of their anniversary. He then strangles her, making it appear that she has met her tragic end at a lover's hands. But, of course, he has a seemingly unshakable alibi. You got it. He has a house full of guests there to celebrate their wedding anniversary who swear that they saw the late Mrs. X slip quietly into the gardens through the French doors but are equally adamant that their host never left the festivities.

Leaving the Boathouse, Katherine wandered through the magnificent gardens as the sweet yet spicy scent of the rhododendrons awoke her senses further. Soon she found herself standing at the front door of Greenway. Stepping over the threshold, Katherine wandered into the drawing-room. Closing her eyes, she could almost picture Agatha dressed in a 50's style flowery summer frock, pacing slowly back and forth in front of the fireplace and gesturing with her hands as she read her newest novel to her gathered family. At the same time, they tried to guess "who done it." It was the summer holiday, and the family gathered here as they did every summer after Agatha finished her latest book.

After a full day of traveling and touring Greenway, Katherine headed over to the Tack Room Takeaway to grab a sandwich and a pastry or two for her evening meal and headed back to the Lodge for an early evening.

Tomorrow was another day, and Katherine planned on an early start to take a swim at Elberry Cove, Agatha's favorite bathing spot, and then back to enjoy lunch at The House Kitchen inside Greenway and perhaps get more ideas for future storylines.

After a quiet evening, Katherine retired only to dream of mystery and murder.

The following day after breakfast, Katherine donned her swimsuit, grabbed my towel and beach bag, and headed down from Greenway through the woods to Elberry Cove. She was anxious to see it because it had featured as the setting of Sir Carmichael Clarke's untimely death in the ABC Murders.

Katherine was delighted to find the small beach deserted, and laying out her towel and beach bag on the shingle beach, she ventured into the clear waters. After swimming for a half hour or so, Katherine decided to explore the remains of Lord Churston's bathhouse. She had read all the tourist information and found it described as a romantic 18th-century ruin. The building was three stories in its hay day, with a thatched roof and a ground floor that would flood when the tide came in. This allowed Lord Churston and his guests to swim straight out into the sea through a gated doorway. The building also boasted an early version of a hot tub, with a fire heating the seawater to warm swimmers after their dip. Such luxuries! She was beginning to feel chilled now as a cloud moved across the sun, and she turned to leave as the ruin took on a more sinister look and a chill crept up her spine. It was then that Katherine noticed the smell. At first, she thought it was the smell of stagnant water and rotting wood, but she soon realized that it was a smell that she knew only too well from her former job…it was the smell of rotting flesh. After twenty years as a police officer, that was a smell you never forgot.

Anxious not to disturb a possible crime scene, Katherine quickly ran to her towel, grabbed her mobile from her beach bag, and dialed 999.

"Do you need the police or an Ambulance?" the operator asked.

"Police, please. I want to report that I believe I have found a dead body."

"Your name, ma'am?"

"Katherine Lambert."

"OK, Ms. Lambert. Did you actually see this dead body?"

"No, but I smelled it."

Katherine heard a slight chuckle from the police operator, and before she could respond, Katherine said, "Listen, after twenty years as a detective with homicide in the MET, I think that I can tell a dead body by its smell. Soon as I smelled it, I left the building. I didn't think your detectives would appreciate me trampling all over a possible crime scene."

Immediately the operator's tone of voice changed, "Yes, ma'am. If you can tell me your location, I'll send a patrol car out to you immediately."

"I'm on the beach at Elberry Cove. I've been staying at Greenway. The victim is in the ruins of Lord Churston's bathhouse. I'll wait here on the beach for their arrival and make sure that no one else enters the bathhouse."

Ending the call, Katherine plopped down on her towel and said to herself, "Why does it seem that death follows me everywhere?"

Less than thirty minutes later, Katherine heard the faint sounds of sirens as the local police approached. Getting to her feet, she wrapped her beach towel around her waist in a skirt-like manner and prepared for their arrival. It wasn't long before two police officers, one in plain clothes, could be seen coming through the wooded vale towards the beach.

"Ms. Lambert, I'm PC Adam Meyers, and this is Detective Inspector Sam Adams. You reported a dead body?"

The PC displaying his warrant card was a freckle-faced, thin young man with a shock of ginger hair. The other officer, older with dark hair and brooding, hooded eyes, turned his face to Katherine and asked, "I believe you told our operator that you believe you found a dead body. Can you show us where you think this alleged victim is located?"

Katherine felt her skin prickle and the hair on the nape of her neck rise. She had dealt with this type of attitude throughout her years with the MET. Perhaps it was because she was younger than most of the officers of her rank, or maybe it was because she was female. Either way, it didn't sit well with Katherine.

"If you search the bathhouse, you'll find a body or what remains of one."

Nodding, the brooding detective turned his back on Katherine without a further word and trudged across the beach to the dilapidated bathhouse. Stopping for just a moment to slip into shoe protectors and don gloves, the two officers disappeared into the dark and dank building. Dropping down onto her blanket, Katherine waited. Fortunately, she didn't have long to wait.

PC Meyers was the first to exit the building as he rushed toward the structure's side and lost what was left of his breakfast in the deep undergrowth. He was quickly followed by Detective Adams, who was talking on his mobile as he walked toward Katherine. Stopping from within a few feet from where Katherine sat wrapped up in her towel, a wet and cold Katherine could just make out him calling for the Scene of Crime Officers and the coroner.

As soon as he ended his call, Katherine climbed to her feet and asked, "I heard you called for SOCO, so I guess you found my alleged victim. May I go now? I'm a bit cold and would like to get out of my wet swimsuit and into some dry clothes?"

"I'll need your details first. Then, we'll need to take a statement from you."

"Yes, I know the procedure. I'm staying at Greenway in the Lodge through the weekend."

Taking his notebook from his pocket, he asked, "Name and address?"

"Katherine Lambert. Formerly of 101 Burwood Road, London."

Raising an eyebrow, the detective asked, "Formerly?"

"Yes, formerly. My flat in London sold quickly, and the new owners needed quick settlement, so I stayed with a work colleague until my retirement, then came straight here. I begin searching for temporary accommodations in the next day or two. I can give you my mobile number, and you can reach me that way. I'll let you know as soon as I get somewhere to stay."

"I understand from our dispatcher that you identified yourself as a homicide detective with the MET," replied the brash detective staring into Kate's eyes.

"Actually, I said I spent 20 years as a homicide detective with the MET, and the title is Detective Chief Inspector."

"Thank you, DCI Lambert. We can work with that."

Kate thought for just a second about telling him that she was no longer an active DCI but decided that would lead to even more questions about her personal life, which was totally unrelated to the case.

As Detective Adams walked towards the path to await the scene of crime officers, the young PC walked over, "Sorry, Miss, but I overheard you say that you are looking for somewhere to live temporarily while house hunting."

"Yes, that's right."

"Well, one of our associates mentioned that they have a holiday let and hope to find a tenant for three or more months. To be perfectly honest, I think they have grown weary of changing the bed linens and cleaning the cottage after every weekly rental. It's close to the water and in a rural position but within walking distance to the village."

"Thank you, PC Myers! I'd love to view the rental. Do you have your associate's phone number so I can contact him?"

Smiling, he looked towards the path at the white overall-clad figure coming towards them, "He's a she, and she's just coming now. Nicki Hopwood is our coroner."

Katherine turned her head to watch as the diminutive blonde carefully made her way down the sloping grade, followed by her photographer assistant.

Stopping to speak with the lead Scene of Crime Officer briefly, the young woman shook her head before signaling to her photographer to get started photographing the crime scene in the bathhouse as she made her way to where PC Myers and Kate waited on the beach.

Smiling brightly, Nicki greeted PC Myers, "Hey Adam, how are you?"

Not waiting for a reply, she turned her attention to Katherine, "I understand you're the one who found the body. Did you touch anything at the crime scene?"

Before Katherine could answer, they were joined by Detective Adams, "I think you'll find that the crime scene has been perfectly preserved. Miss Lambert is a Detective Chief Inspector of Homicide with the MET."

Nicki shook hands with Katherine, extending her hand, "Pleasure to meet you, Detective Chief Inspector."

Katherine shook her hand, smiling, "Nice to meet you, and it's just plan, Kate. I hear that you may be looking for a tenant."

"Yes, I am. Give me your number, and I'll arrange to show you the cottage."

"This is my mobile number," Kate recited her number before adding, "I'll be staying here in the Lodge at Greenway for the next couple of days."

Smiling, Nicki replied, "How about this evening? I'll call you later and arrange a time to pick you up."

"That would be wonderful since I don't have a car yet."

After saving Kate's phone number into her mobile, Nicki turned to Detective Adams, "OK, let's get this over. I hear it's rather grim."

Chapter 3

It wasn't until later that evening when Coroner Nicki Hopwood collected Kate for the short drive to her home outside the village of Galmpton that Kate found out just how grim her discovery had been. As Nicki maneuvered her Mini down the narrow country lanes brushing against the hedgerows, Kate made a mental note to look at only compact cars when the time came to purchase.

Nicki finally pulled off the road and drove down a short tree-lined drive arriving at a stone, and thatched cottage, explaining, "Right across from my drive is a bus stop. It can get you into Brixham in less than 10 minutes. You can find a lot of what you'll need there."

Climbing out of her car, Nicki smiled and said, "It's been a long day. It always seems longer when it's your first day back from holiday. Let's have a glass of wine before I show you the rental."

"Sounds perfect," said Kate, admiring the neat flower-laden gardens and lush foliage. The location certainly looked idyllic.

Entering through the heavy oak door, the first room to greet Kate was a low beamed cozy sitting room anchored at the far end by a vast stone inglenook open fire, complete with a bread oven. Kate's eyes swept the room and smiled at Nicki's taste in furnishings. Everything tied together perfectly, and the cottage was immaculate. Nicki was obviously house-proud and spent much of her spare time at home.

"This is charming," exclaimed Kate!

"Thank you. It's been in the family for years. During my grandmother's time, it had been two farm worker's cottages. She had more children than the single cottage could comfortably accommodate, so when next door became vacant, grandfather bought it, and it was knocked thru into one large cottage."

Turning right, Nicki led the way into a cozy kitchen/diner and asked, "Red or White?"

"White would be lovely."

Nicki smiled, grabbed the wine, and pointed to the table, "Have a seat, and I'll get some glasses."

Soon as they were seated at the table, Nicki poured the wine and took a large drink of hers, "After that autopsy today, I needed this. Normally, I don't drink much, but this was one of the most gruesome I've seen. Of course, we get some car accidents, drownings, and just questionable deaths, but not many murders and mutilations. But, I guess you see more of that working for the MET."

"Unfortunately, yes, that was one of the reasons why I retired so young," replied Kate

"Oh, I wasn't aware you had retired. You're so young; I just assumed that you might be looking for a holiday home," replied Nicki before she suddenly noticed the sad look that came over Kate's face. Nicki recognized that she had unknowingly upset her visitor and quickly reached over and covered Kate's hand with hers, "I'm sorry. I've said something to upset you. I didn't mean to pry into your personal business."

Tilting back her head and emptying her glass, Kate said, "That's alright. Can I see the rental now?"

Pushing her chair back and rising to her feet with a smile, Nicki walked a few feet and opened a door as she explained, "This door connects to the holiday let, but it can be locked from both sides, so you have complete privacy. There's a separate entry at the side of the house right in front of a parking place for when you get a car."

Upon opening the door, Kate's eyes first lighted on the compact but beautifully fitted kitchen. Through the kitchen was a large room that held a small dining table, sofa, and two chairs. Against the far wall was a wood burner for those chilly evenings.

Nicki continued the tour by saying, "There's a utility room and loo off the kitchen and two bedrooms and a family bath upstairs if you follow me."

Leading the way, Nicki pointed to the bath at the top of the staircase, "There's both a shower and bath with a soaking tub. When I had one added to my bath, I asked the installers to install one in the rental. People seem to love these antique-looking soaking tubs. I must admit that I enjoy a good soak after a long day bending over a dead body on a slab. Of course, the glass of wine I'm drinking while soaking in the lovely scented bubble bath helps too," laughed Nicki before continuing, "The bedrooms are on either side of the bath and are both doubles."

A beaming Kate turned to Nicki, "This is just what I've been hoping to find. Could I ask what the monthly rent will be?"

"I'm glad you like it. Would you be willing to do your own cleaning and laundry?"

"Yes, of course."

Nicki sighed with relief, "Thank goodness! I don't mind telling you that renting the cottage out for a weekend or week at a time was wearing me out, all that constant cleaning and laundering of bedding and towels. On the other hand, the holiday let business is great if you don't have a full-time job where you can get called out day or night. Well, let's see, do you think 800 pounds a month is too high?"

It was well below what Kate was expecting to have to pay. "That sounds more than fair. When can I move in?"

Relieved that Kate had liked the arrangement, Nicki replied, "Is Sunday soon enough? I can pick you up when you are due to check out of Greenway and take you into Brixham so you can pick up any food or other necessities."

"That would be great, but I don't want to be a bother. I could take the bus."

"It's not a bother, I have to go anyway and do my weekly shop, and I'd be glad for the company."

Heading into her cottage, Nicki said, "I better be getting you back. I have an early start tomorrow."

It wasn't until they were on the road back to Greenway that Kate ventured to ask, "You mentioned murder and mutilation. I didn't see the victim, so I thought perhaps it was a case of misadventure."

"I think that's what we all assumed until we saw the corpse. I'm sure you're aware I shouldn't be discussing the case, but I don't see any harm in telling you, all things considered."

"I quite understand. You don't have to discuss the case if it makes you uncomfortable."

"No, it's all right. Besides, I think our gorgeous detective might be stopping by at some point to try to draw on your experience. Well, it seems that our victim was missing his hands and head. So, definitely, not a drowning or boating accident. He'd been in the water for a few days, so the fish had been at him. The preliminary exam was done today, but the real work starts tomorrow."

Kate had witnessed many killings like this, and in almost all cases, they were gang executions, something not uncommon in a large metropolitan area. Still, here in rural Devon, it was a rarity.

Chapter 4

Kate had barely seated herself in the Lodge's small lounge with a steaming cup of tea at her side when a thunderous knock on the front door had her jumping to her feet. Throwing open the door, she came face-to-face with the grim, frowning face of Detective Sam Adams. Not waiting to be invited in, the detective strode into the lounge, "This is the third time I've had to come back up here. I thought I advised you that I needed to take your statement."

"I must apologize. I thought you knew Ms. Hopwood was taking me to see her rental this evening. I've just returned," replied Kate.

"No, I wasn't aware you would be leaving the premises. I'm sure you're well aware from your background that getting a witness statement as soon as possible is always preferable while it's still fresh in their minds."

"Well, since I didn't actually witness the crime or, for that matter, even see the deceased's remains, I assumed that it wasn't urgent. And may I remind you that you didn't say that you wanted to take my statement today," snapped Kate.

Noticing that the detective's eyes were staring in the direction of her steaming cup of tea, Kate calmed down and said, "I was just having a cup of tea. Can I get you a coffee or tea while we get this interview out of the way?"

"Tea would be very welcome. It's been a long day," replied Sam as he followed Kate into the small kitchen and stood looming in the doorway.

Looking over her shoulder at the exhausted man, Kate said, "Oh, for goodness sake, do have a seat in the lounge by the fire. You're making me nervous looming there. I'll bring in the tea."

Fixing a tray with the tea, milk, and sugar and some custard creams she had brought from London, Kate rejoined the detective in the lounge.

As Kate poured the tea and handed a cup to Sam, she asked, "So, any leads yet?"

Almost choking on his first sip of the hot brew, the detective said, "Actually, Ms. Lambert, it is Miss, isn't it? I believe I'm supposed to be asking you the questions."

Ignoring his question regarding her marital status, Kate chuckled before replying, "Point well taken, Detective. Sometimes I forget that I'm no longer the investigator."

Just nodding and drinking his tea, Sam finally raised his eyes from his cup and stared into Kate's eyes before asking, "Did you deal with many murders involving mutilation while with the MET?"

Avoiding his stare, Kate realized that Nicki knew the detective very well. She had been right when she said he would stop by to pick her brains.

"More than I care to remember, Detective Adams. Like your body, quite a few of them ended up dumped into the Thames or some other body of water."

Reaching for a custard cream, Sam waved it around in the air as he tried to formulate his next question.

"You know, at first, I thought perhaps it was a boating accident. Sometimes a propeller can cause severe injuries, but when we uncovered the corpse and saw that both hands and head were missing, I knew we were looking at a ruthless murder."

Grabbing a biscuit, Kate leaned back in her chair and tucked her legs under her, "That's where you may be mistaken. It's still basically a suspicious death. We don't know if the victim was murdered."

"Well, from the state of him, I can't think what else it could have been. It's not likely he did it to himself," remarked Sam as he stared open-mouth at Kate.

"I know this may seem very strange to you, but during my time at the MET, we had two cases where the victim appeared to have been murdered. It turned out that the poor sods had, in fact, committed suicide, and because most insurance policies wouldn't pay out for suicide, the families tried to disguise the deaths as murder."

"But surely, they wouldn't dismember a loved one like this victim, " Sam remarked.

"Not to that extent, perhaps. One of our victims had cut his wrists, so the family removed his hands from above the cuts before giving him a river burial. And don't always assume that the loved one, as you call him, was loved by his family. Statistics tell us that family members commit more murders than random strangers."

Shaking his head, Sam replied, "I would never have initially gone down that route. We'll have to wait to see if Nicki comes up with a DNA screen and try to locate his family."

"DNA may take a while to come back. Most victims have something distinguishable, a birthmark, tattoo, scar, or even something as small as a mole. I'm sure Nicki will note any distinguishing marks in the autopsy report. If this were my case, I'd check the missing person reports until more evidence is available."

Taking it all in, Detective Adams nodded and quickly changed the subject, "How did your viewing of Nicki's holiday let go?"

"Very well. It's a beautiful cottage, and the location is ideal. After the weekend here, I'll be moving in there," replied a smiling Kate.

"I couldn't agree more. It's a lovely cottage. I tried renting it from Nicki when she first said she was tired of the holiday letting business, but I don't think she fancied having a work colleague right next door. I live in town now, and although it's close to the sea and amenities, I think I'd prefer something a bit more rural and peaceful."

Rising to his feet and making his way towards the door, Sam said, "Well, thank you for the tea, and I'll be in touch if we need to ask you any further questions."

Watching him walk down the path and returning his wave as he turned back to look at her, Kate thought, "Yes, I just bet you will."

Chapter 5

The rest of Kate's weekend was pleasant but uneventful. Still, the gruesome discovery in the bathhouse had put a damper on her visit to Greenway, leaving her eagerly anticipating the move to her new home.

Coroner Nicki Hopwood picked up Kate just as she had promised first thing on Sunday and made the short drive into Brixham to pick up a few necessities for the cottage. As they drove down the narrow lanes, Kate asked, "Any luck on identifying the remains yet?"

Nicki slowed down and pulled over close to the hedgerow as a lorry came trundling down the narrow lane facing them. Kate's sharp intake of breath made Nicki giggle, "This is something you'll have to get used to if you're planning on driving here. I guess you don't have this kind of problem in London. My advice is, get a compact car."

Exhaling as the lorry passed within inches of Nicki's car, Kate breathed a sigh of relief when Nicki pulled back out and answered her question. "I got lucky with the identification. It seems the victim must have broken his femur in the past. Since 1990, manufacturers are required to number implanted orthopedic devices allowing the identification process when traditional methods fail."

"So, you know who the victim is?" asked Kate.

Nicki had reached the town center, and as she maneuvered into a parking spot, she turned to Kate and replied, "The device is registered to a John-James Granville,"

"Is he a local?" asked Kate.

"Yes, but this is where it gets a bit tricky, he's a Crown Prosecutor, so I'm assuming the locals will have to call in the Met to assist."

"Has the next of kin been notified?"

"I understand that our gorgeous, mysterious Detective Adams will see them later today."

Climbing out of the Mini, Kate asked, "Why do you keep referring to him like that?"

"Well, he is gorgeous and very mysterious with it. He doesn't seem to notice any of many available females who hang on his every word."

"Well, maybe he's gay and not interested," replied Kate.

"Nope, I don't think so. Call me a romantic, but I think he's had his heart broken and is leery of any further romantic involvement."

Thinking about her recent loss, Kate quietly replied, "I can completely understand that."

Realizing she had again broached a painful subject with her new friend, Nicki placed her hand on Kate's arm, "I hope we can be good friends, and if I say something that causes you discomfort or pain, it's because I don't know anything about your past to avoid talking about."

Smiling and nodding, Kate linked her arm through Nicki's, "I'd like that very much. Is there a good tea shop around? I've heard so much about these Devon Cream Teas that I've been dying to try one."

The tea shop was just as Kate imagined. Teapots hung from hooks from the ceiling, and beautiful mismatched place settings adorned the white table-clothed tables. When Kate's phone rang, they had just begun delving into the scones and clotted cream with homemade strawberry preserves. Pulling it out of her pocket, she frowned as she immediately recognized the phone number as that of her former boss, Commander Morgan.

Looking across at Nicki, who was busy spreading the clotted cream on her scone, Kate apologized as she stood up and stepped away from the table, "Sorry, I'm afraid that I have to take this."

Nicki just nodded and continued adding the strawberry jam before taking a satisfying bite,

"Sir, what can I do for you?"

"How are you settling in, Lambert?"

"Fine, Sir, I've managed to find a cottage to rent next door to the local coroner."

"Yes, so I've heard."

Kate laughed, "Are you keeping tabs on me, Sir?"

"No, I wasn't until I had a call from a certain Detective down there informing me that you had discovered the body of Crown Prosecutor John-James Granville and that you were very helpful with their investigation. So valuable in fact that he has requested that you be allowed to assist in the investigation."

"I told him I was no longer with the Met, so I don't understand."

"Technically, you are still with the MET. Your medical leave paperwork hasn't gone through yet, so you're still on the payroll. But, I have another reason for considering his request. One of the last cases that Granville

29

prosecuted was against an affiliate of Igor Smolenski. We also believe he may have given the orders for the ambush that cost Detective Sanders his life."

"I'm with someone now, Sir. Can I phone you back in a few hours?"

"Yes, but don't make it too long. Detective Adams hopes you will be available to accompany him to interview the widow later today."

"I'll speak to you soon," replied Kate as she ended the call and returned to the table.

Noticing Kate's mood change, Nicki asked, "Is everything alright? I hope it's not bad news."

"It seems my retirement hasn't gone through yet, and I've been assigned a new case."

"Oh no! Don't tell me that you're leaving us so soon."

"No, even worse. I've been assigned to the Devon constabulary to work the Granville murder with Detective Adams."

Still munching away, Nicki replied, "I knew that the MET would get involved, and I'm not surprised he asked for you."

"Really? Why do you say that?" asked Kate as she finally took a bite from her scone and moaned in delight.

Laughing, Nicki said, "Good, aren't they?"

"The best! I could live on these alone, but I'm afraid my waistline might suffer!"

"Back to your question, Sam was waxing lyrical about how brilliant you were when he stopped in at the morgue to check on the autopsy progress."

"Oh, he was, was he?"

"I referred to the victim as a murder victim, and he quickly told me that at the moment, he was treating it as a suspicious death. Then he related something about mutilation to mask a suicide, which would prevent insurance payout. I figured that you might have mentioned that."

"I did indeed. We ran across a few of those in London during my time there."

Tilting her head to one side, Nicki asked, "So, what are you going to do?"

Kate's eyes clouded over, "Based on what the Commander just told me, I have no choice. I must see this case through to the end."

After a quick shop, Nicki dropped Kate off at the cottage and left her to return her call to Commander Morgan.

Once Kate had confirmed the details, she punched in the number of Detective Adam's mobile and, without even saying hello, said, "What time are you picking me up?"

"I'll be there in an hour if that's convenient for you."

"Let's get one thing straight. Nothing about this deal is convenient for me," Kate retorted as she disconnected the call.

Chapter 6

Kate was looking out the window, waiting for Detective Sam Adams to pull into her drive. There was no way that she wanted to welcome him into her cottage. A cottage that Kate knew from their previous conversation that he coveted. As soon as he pulled up, she grabbed her suit coat and was out the door before he could even exit the driver's seat.

Slipping into the passenger seat, she fastened her seatbelt and, looking straight ahead, asked, "Where are we going?"

Trying to make eye contact with her, Sam said, "To notify the next of kin. I thought I had told you."

"No, Commander Morgan told me, and another thing, you'll find me a lot less cooperative next time you decide to go over my head to my boss. Do you understand?"

"Yes, I'm sorry about that. The MET had to be notified, and because you discovered the body, I mistakenly thought you would be interested in following through on it."

"Well, I wasn't, so let's get this wrapped up as quick as possible so I can get on with my retirement."

Just nodding as he put the car into reverse, he continued, "We are heading to Millstone Manor, the Granville family home. I spoke to his office, and they said that Mrs. Granville was to drop her husband at the train station four days ago to go to a friend's home in Scotland for a grouse shoot. That explains why no one has reported him missing."

"Doesn't it seem odd that the friend in Scotland didn't call when Granville failed to arrive?" asked Kate.

"It did cross my mind. Isn't it customary for the wife to call and check that her husband arrived safely?" asked Sam.

"How would I know? I've never been married. Maybe they didn't have that kind of relationship, or he called, and she was away from home. I guess we'll find out the answer to that question when we interview her," quipped Kate.

"That's a good point. We'll need to delve into Mrs. Granville's relationship with her husband. See if there is any reason why she'd want him dead."

"I agree that everyone is a suspect at this time, but first, we have to break the news that her husband won't be coming home," replied Kate.

The two detectives completed the rest of the journey in silence until Sam turned between the two large granite pillars that marked the entrance to Millstone Manor. The drive curved through what had once been a deer park lined with tall oak trees on either side. The actual manor house stood upon a slight rise above a meandering stream.

Kate's eyes widened, and her mouth dropped open at the sight of the stunning house, "I didn't realize that Crown Prosecutors made enough money to afford something like this. I think a background check of his finances may well be in order."

Sam muttered as he stared across the vast manicured gardens that trailed down past a stable block towards the stream below, "I agree. The maintenance alone must cost a fortune."

Parking in the gravel drive of the house, they approached the front door and knocked on the substantial oak door. Within minutes, an older woman opened the door. Holding up his warrant card, Sam asked, "Mrs. Granville?"

Suppressing a giggle, the older lady said, "No, I'm the housekeeper. Is she expecting you?"

Kate quickly replied, "No, but it is important that we speak with her."

As her smile turned to a frown, the housekeeper said, "Come in, please. I'll tell her you're here."

Trying to wipe a smirk off her face, Kate whispered to Sam, "Obviously, you don't know how the other half lives."

A door to a room off the foyer opened, and an elegantly dressed lady approached them smiling, "I suppose this is about the annual fundraiser."

Kate took the lead, "I'm afraid not. I'm afraid we have some very bad news for you. Is there somewhere that we can speak in private?"

Becoming flustered, she waved them into the room that was obviously a library and quickly asked, "Nothing's happened to the twins, has there? They just took the car for a drive to the coast."

"No, ma'am. I'm afraid this is about your husband."

Showing a mother's relief, Mrs. Granville quickly added, "John's away in Scotland at the moment."

"I'm very sorry to have to tell you this, but your husband's body was discovered two days ago in the boathouse at Greenway. I am very sorry for your loss," said Sam.

Unable to take the news in, the older lady shook her head, "That can't be right. There must be some mistake. I personally put him on the train myself."

"When was the last time you spoke with your husband?" asked Kate gently.

Wringing her hands, she replied, "When I dropped him off at the train station. John didn't like being disturbed while hunting at his friend's estate in Scotland. Every year it was the same routine, I would drop him off at the train station, and he would telephone me when he was preparing to return so I could meet him at the train."

"Did you see him get on the train?"

Becoming more flustered, the older woman replied, "No, it was windy and raining that morning, and John just had me pull up beside the station. He said he didn't want me to ruin my new hairdo. John is always very thoughtful about things like that. He kissed me goodbye, and that's the last I saw him as he waved and entered the station."

Kate quickly noticed that Mrs. Granville was going into shock and promptly told Sam, "Find that housekeeper and get her to bring tea in here and lots of sugar. Mrs. Granville has had quite a shock."

Sam didn't have far to go since the housekeeper was standing right outside the door listening to what everyone was saying inside the library.

Quickly regaining her composure when Sam opened the door, nearly colliding with her, she said, "If you come with me, sir. I'll get you that tea." As they entered the kitchen, she turned to Sam and asked calmly, "Is it true? Is he really dead?"

"I'm afraid so," replied Sam as he waited for the tea tray.

Sam waited a minute before asking, "How long have you worked for the family?"

"Long enough to know all their secrets. If you need any information about what goes on in this house, you just need to ask me," she replied.

He took out his notepad and asked, "Your name, ma'am, and your contact details."

"Eliza Roberts and I live at Oakview cottage just down the road from the entrance here. I am usually home by 9 pm."

Once she had given him the information, the housekeeper handed him the tray and dropped heavily into the worn wooden chair by the Aga, "God rest his soul. He'll be missed by some of us, anyway," she whispered just loud enough for Sam to hear.

When he returned to the library, Sam found Kate sitting beside a now weeping Mrs. Granville. Quickly, reaching for the teapot and pouring the grieving widow a cup of tea, Kate added three rounded teaspoons of sugar and held it out to Mrs. Granville.

"Are you aware of any recent threats against your husband?" asked Sam.

Wiping her eyes and taking a sip of tea, she replied, "Only the usual. It seemed like every time John got a conviction; the criminal acted like it was John's fault that he was being sent down and would threaten revenge. John just said that it all went with the territory. He never seemed to take it seriously."

Still pressing, Sam asked, "Anything recently that you recall? Any change in your husband's moods or behavior?"

"No, actually, he was in a cheerful mood. He couldn't wait to go off to Scotland shooting."

Placing her hand over the widow's hand, Kate said, "We will need the name and contact details for his friend in Scotland."

"Yes, of course. I'll get his details for you," Mrs. Granville replied as she walked over to her husband's desk by the window.

"I know I already asked, but I just need to confirm that you didn't speak with your husband while he was away," asked Kate.

"No, John hated being bothered while he was away. He always said it was his time to unwind. I've never even met or spoken to his friend. I only know that they were old schoolmates."

The sound of a car parking on the gravel drive sent Mrs. Granville to the floor-to-ceiling sash window that faced the drive. "It's the twins, David and Douglas. How can I tell them that their father isn't coming home?"

Before Kate could answer, two identical young men in their early twenties came bounding into the library.

"Sorry to interrupt, mother. We didn't know you had company," said David as they began backing out of the room.

Trying to remain calm for her children, the new widow explained, "These are the police, and they've come about your father."

Douglas laughed heartily," What's the old scoundrel been up to now?" as he poked his brother in the ribs with his elbow.

At this point, Kate took over, "I'm afraid we've just given your mother some very bad news. Perhaps you'd like to sit down."

As soon as the twins seated themselves on either side of their mother, she continued, "A body, identified as belonging to your father, was recovered from the River Dart two days ago."

The reactions from the twins couldn't have been more different. David looked shocked and immediately put his hands over his face as he openly wept. Douglas, in contrast, jumped to his feet, "There has to be some mistake! Father is in Scotland for a shoot. If it was him and I stress the word 'if,' then why has it taken you two days to notify us? It's not like his face hasn't been all over the papers lately."

This question was the one question that both detectives dreaded having to answer. It was hard enough to tell a grieving family that their loved one was dead but harder still that he was murdered and his body mutilated.

Sam quickly looked to the more experienced Kate as she said, "As we explained, your father's body was found in the River Dart. When bodies are in the water for any amount of time, it makes identification much harder."

Douglas seemed to accept her explanation and sat back down before placing a comforting arm around his mother's shoulders.

"We'll need to speak with both of you later, so stay in the area," said Sam.

This remark had Douglas back on his feet and in Sam's face, "What kind of sons do you think we are? Do you really think we would leave our mother at a time like this? Wait, are you inferring that one of us had something to do with our father's death?"

Kate stepped in between the two men and defused the situation. "Of course not. We're just hoping that you might be able to help us bring your father's murderer to justice. You may have noticed changes in your father's behavior or heard something that might now make more sense. We won't bother you anymore today. Once again, we are very sorry for your loss."

Nodding at Sam, they turned to leave. As they approached the door, David touched Kate's shoulder, "There was something, but I didn't want to mention it in front of mother. A month or so ago, I skipped out on my classes to take this girl I was trying to impress to the Savoy for tea. We were just leaving when I saw him."

Kate stared into the boy's concerned eyes, "Who did you see, David?"

"It was Dad. He was getting on the elevator with this blond. He had his hand on her ass."

"Are you quite sure it was your father?"

"Yes, I was almost certain, but I was still hoping I was wrong, so I called his office and asked for Dad, and they said he was in London for a meeting."

"Can you describe the woman he was with a little better?"

"She was dressed in a blue suit and was kind of short. I remember because she was wearing what the guys call hooker heels, and she still was a lot shorter than Dad.

40

Oh, and she had short blond hair. Their backs were to me, so that's all I can tell you, sorry."

Patting him on the shoulder, Kate smiled into his troubled eyes and said, "I think you've done quite well. Thank you."

"Do you have a card, so I can reach you if we think of anything in the meantime?"

"Of course, handing him the card, he looked down at it before saying, "I didn't realize that the MET was handling Dad's death."

Kate gave the young man a sympathetic smile and, patting him on the shoulder, said, "We'll be in touch. Look out for your mum. She's had a horrible shock."

Chapter 7

Once they had driven to the end of the long drive, Sam turned right instead of left, which would have taken them back to Kate's cottage. Before Kate could question him, he remarked, "While I was getting the tea from Mrs. Roberts, she told me her cottage was up this way."

Raising her eyebrows, Kate said, "I didn't take her for your type. It just goes to show, doesn't it?"

"Don't be daft. The old girl told me that if I really wanted to know what goes on at Millstone Manor, I should talk to her," replied Sam as he slowed the car and pointed to a small cottage set among some oak trees. The sign beside the door proclaimed that it was Oakview Cottage.

"We'll need to stop by and see her later this evening after she gets off work at 9:00. Something about the family dynamic has me curious."

Raising her eyebrows again, Kate replied, "Really, I thought they behaved perfectly normal for people who have just been told their loved one has been murdered. But, I'm sure you are a better judge of local people than I am."

Turning the car around in the cottages' drive, Sam headed back towards Kate's. Kate spied a pub ahead when they were within a half-mile of home.

"Have you eaten?" Kate quickly asked.

"No, do you want to stop?"

"Yes, I missed breakfast, and I've wanted to check out this pub anyway. It's close enough to walk to if I decide I want a few pints before going home."

Pulling into the car park, Sam chuckled.

"What's so funny?" asked Kate.

"I was just picturing you sitting at the bar lifting a few pints with the locals."

"What's so funny about that?"

"I don't know. I picture you in some classy wine bar in London sipping some overly expensive wine."

Unbuckling her seat belt and climbing out of the car, Kate thought, *He sure doesn't know me very well.*

Sam held the door open for Kate as they entered what was appropriately named the Old Forge Inn. The whole side wall now featured a massive fireplace that had once served the forge. Heading to a table close to the warm fire, Kate plopped down as Sam headed for the bar. At the bar, Sam called over, "What can I get you?"

"Make mine a pint of their best local ale."

Putting the two pints on the table, Sam passed Kate a menu, and the two detectives sat in silence while they sipped their ale and made their selections from the menu.

A young pony-tailed waitress approached the table within minutes, "Are you ready to order?"

Sam waved a hand at Kate, allowing Kate to order first. "I'll have the beef and ale pie with chips, please."

"And you, sir?"

"I'll have the Ploughman's."

Kate waited until the waitress had walked away before saying, "Lovely, guess I'll get to smell pickled onion breath the entire drive back to my house."

Leaning back in his chair, Sam lifted his pint to his lips and then stopped before saying, "It's only a ten-minute drive to your cottage, and you can keep the windows down, but if that is objectionable, then you can always walk home. Cheers!"

Kate couldn't help but smile as she raised her glass and said, "Cheers." Kate liked a partner she could banter with, someone with grit, and she felt that she and Sam could work well together.

The food arrived, and Kate laughed when she saw that the Ploughman's platter didn't come with the usual pickled onion.

"Something funny," asked Sam?"

"Yes, no pickled onion!"

"I'm a regular here, and the waitress knows that I can't stand pickled onion, so it never comes with my Ploughman's," replied Sam before finishing his pint and hungrily attacking the plate of thick-sliced gammon and cheddar.

"Hope this pie is as good as it looks. My mum used to make pastry like this, but I've never been able to master the art," said Kate as she tucked into her meal.

"It's an art, like baking bread. My Aunt Mildred makes the most delicious loaves of bread. I never eat store-bought if I can help it. I can bring you a loaf whenever you need some if you like." replied Sam.

"That would be much appreciated," said Kate, lowering her head and concentrating on the heavenly pie in front of her.

It was Sam's turn to laugh, "Who would have thought that we would be sitting here discussing our mutual love of home-baked bread when we're supposed to be solving a murder."

"Well, I believe Napoleon said that an army travels on its stomach and our army of two needs feeding too," said Kate.

The two detectives arrived back at Kate's cottage an hour later, stomachs full.

"We still have a couple of hours before we speak with Eliza Roberts. Do you want to go over what we know now before we question her?" asked Sam as he turned off the ignition key.

Shrugging her shoulders, Kate said, "We don't really know much yet but come on in, and we can at least compare our perspectives of the Granvilles."

Kate immediately went to the Aga and set the kettle on to brew some tea while Sam slumped into the lounge chair.

Carrying the tray laden with tea, cream, and sugar into the lounge, Kate found that Sam had nodded off and was softly snoring. There were still two hours left before Mrs. Roberts would finish work and possibly return home, so she decided to let Sam nap. As he slept, his face relaxed, and he took on the appearance of a much younger man. Kate wondered how old he was and what had happened in his past for him to be so cynical. Kate enjoyed finding out what made people behave the way they do, and Sam's story was another mystery that Kate hoped to solve.

An hour later, Kate gently poked Sam, who looked around as if he couldn't quite remember where he was. Kate said, handing him a cup of newly brewed tea, "Mrs. Roberts should be back home in about an hour. We still have time to review our thoughts on the Granvilles and correlate any questions we want to ask the housekeeper."

Sputtering Sam, "I'm sorry. I don't know what got into me. I must have dozed off as soon as I sat down."

"I can tell you. You're exhausted. If you go on the way you have, you'll burn out and be no good to anyone. Believe me, the last thing I want is a partner I can't depend on because he is sleep-deprived."

Gulping his tea, Sam replied, "Yes, Boss."

Turning her back on Sam and walking back into her kitchen, Kate muttered, "And just remember that."

Chapter 8

"While you were napping, I placed a call to that so-called old buddy in Scotland. Not only was he not expecting the victim, but Granville has not been welcomed in his home since he showed up with a tart in tow, not my word but the good Colonel's, some five years ago."

"So the question is where has he been going these last five years, and who is the tart, I mean lady, in question?"

"Well, it's not something we can delicately ask the grieving widow, now can we? Maybe Mrs. Roberts will be able to enlighten us on that point," said Kate.

Reaching for his mobile, Sam said, "I'll get on the team and have them check the train station to see where Granville was actually going that day."

"If it turns out to be London, I'll have my team at the MET check the surveillance cameras leading from the station on the day in question. If we get lucky, we can find whoever he was meeting, or if not, where he was going. If he's been getting away with this for five years, I don't think he will be cautious about covering his tracks."

After completing their calls, Sam asked, "Did the Colonel know who this other woman was?"

"Only that she was much younger, blond, and fit. He could be describing any number of women."

"Didn't he notice anything else that was different about her?"

"Now that you mention it. The Colonel did say that the woman in question had a beauty mark just above her lip."

"What the hell is a beauty mark," asked Sam.

Laughing, Kate said, "Basically, it's a mole on the face."

Sam shrugged his shoulders, "Well, that should narrow it down just a little bit. We'll see if Mrs. Roberts knows of anyone meeting that description."

Looking down at her wristwatch, Kate said, "Speaking of Mrs. Roberts, we better get moving if we want to catch her before she turns in for the night. I have a feeling that the good housekeeper is early to bed and early to rise."

When the two detectives arrived at Oakview Cottage, the lights were on, and smoke rose from the chimney despite it being summer. Knocking on the door, they were greeted by Mrs. Roberts and invited into her lounge, where a wood stove was blazing away.

"I hope it isn't too warm for you. I know it's summer and all, but this old cottage gets cold quickly sitting under the shade of these big oaks, and the older you get, the more you feel even the slightest cold."

Sam smiled assuredly, "No problem at all, Mrs. Roberts. I love a nice fire, and it still gets chilly in the evening."

"I was just going to have a glass of wine. Would either of you like to join me?"

"That sounds wonderful," replied Kate.

"And you, Detective Adams? Can I tempt you?" asked the older woman.

"Thank you, but no. I'm driving, and it wouldn't do for me to be cautioned for driving over the limit."

"Suit yourself," she replied over her shoulder, and she went into the kitchen to retrieve the glasses and a bottle of white wine.

As soon as everyone was comfortable, Sam mentioned their conversation earlier today in the kitchen at Millpond Manor,

"Mrs. Roberts, you seem to allude to the fact that everyone might not miss Mr. Granville. Would you care to elaborate on that?"

"As long as what I tell you remains confidential. I wouldn't want to lose my position there. If the family decides to keep me on after all this."

Kate looked confused by the last remark and asked, "Why would Mrs. Granville terminate your employment just because her husband has died? I would think that she would need your help more at a time like this."

Taking a long sip of her wine and reaching for the bottle before topping up her glass, Mrs. Roberts said, "Because I know too much."

Sam leaned forward in his seat and asked, "What exactly do you know that might be relevant to our investigation of Mr. Granville's murder?"

"For one, he wasn't going to no grouse shoot in Scotland, and I am pretty sure his wife knew it. And if she knew it, maybe the boys did too. Those two boys are mama boys. They never got on much with their father. He was a busy man and never had time for them as a real father does, but he sure had time for his other interests," smirked the old housekeeper.

"What other interests might you be referring to, Mrs. Roberts," asked Kate.

The old woman snorted, "Other women, of course, and the younger, the better as far as he was concerned."

Kate nodded towards Sam before asking, "And you are sure that his wife knew about these other women?"

"Oh yeah, didn't I hear them with my own ears arguing about it? It is a wonder that half the neighbors didn't hear her the way she was screaming."

"When was this, Mrs. Roberts?"

"Let me see. The last big flare-up was about a month ago. I couldn't help but laugh. She, of all people, called him a degenerate. Talk about the pot calling the kettle black."

Kate cocked her head to one side and asked, "Are you trying to tell me that Mrs. Granville's behavior wasn't exactly above board?"

"Above board, that's a laugh. The Mrs. was having it off with the gardener and him being just a bit older than the twins. I wish I'd told her husband, but I kept my mouth shut. Jobs are hard to come by when you get my age, and a person has to eat."

Drink too, thought Kate as the housekeeper filled up her third glass of wine.

Sam asked, "Do you have any idea who this last woman Mr. Granville might have been seeing is?"

"Nope, not a clue, but you might want to speak to his secretary. She makes all his travel arrangements, so she might be able to give you some idea of where he goes on the odd weekend."

Standing to leave, they thanked the housekeeper for her information, promising to keep it confidential. As she turned to latch the front gate, Kate spied the old lady pouring the leftover wine from Kate's glass into her glass.

Nudging Sam, Kate said, "I think our Mrs. Roberts may have a drinking problem, or she just really likes her wine."

"And I think we had better check the alibis for everyone living and working at Millstone Manor just as soon as Nicki can give up a better estimate of time of death. It seems like a lot of them may have motives for murder," replied Sam.

It was getting late by the time Sam dropped Kate back at her cottage, arranging to pick her up in the morning to pay a visit to the office of the late Crown Prosecutor.

Chapter 9

The next day dawned cloudy with a threat of rain when a knock on her door brought Kate jumping out of bed and reaching for her robe before thundering down the steps from her upstairs bedroom. Throwing open the front door, she was surprised to find no one there. Then, she realized the knocking was coming from the adjoining cottage door. Throwing open the door, she was greeted by a fresh-faced and smiling Nicki, holding two steaming mugs of tea.

"I was afraid I might have awakened you, so I come with gifts," beamed Nicki.

Ushering Nicki into her cottage, Kate grabbed the cup of tea and waved Nicki to a chair in the lounge.

"I wanted to catch you before Sam got here. I finally have a more accurate time of death. The victim died between the hours of 10 pm and 1 am three days before your discovery of the remains."

"So, that would mean that he died two days after his wife claims to have dropped him off at the train station," calculated Kate.

Nicki replied, taking a sip of her tea., "That sounds right. Wait, did you just say that his wife claims? Is she a suspect now?"

"Ah, Nicki, you know how this plays out. Everyone is a suspect until eliminated. We still need to ascertain the family's movements leading to Granville's murder. We found out last night that not everything at Millstone Manor was all sunshine and roses."

"Oh, marital discord, huh?"

"Yeah, big time. It appears that the very respectable Crown Prosecutor was a habitual cheater, and his wife allegedly is having an affair with the much younger gardener. Add to that, his sons were not his biggest fans and were very protective of their mother."

"Good grief! Well, they say money can't buy happiness. I have worked with Granville on many cases, and to be honest, I never got the impression that he was a philanderer. At least he never hit on me."

Kate smiled at the wide-eyed Nicki and said, "Well, that does surprise me because you would be just his type based on what we've heard."

"Now, I don't know whether to be glad that he didn't make a pass or insulted," snickered Nicki.

Looking over at the mantel clock, Nicki drained the last tea from her cup and rose to leave, "Keep me updated. I need to get down to the office, and you need to get dressed, or you'll be entertaining our handsome detective in your nighties."

Kate laughed as she shouted, "That will be the day!"

Locking the adjoining door between the two cottages, Kate flew up the stairs for a quick shower. She had just finished dressing when she heard Sam's car pull in the drive.

Hair still damp, she flung open the front door and was greeted by Sam holding a bag.

Standing on tiptoes, Kate tried to peek in the bag, "I hope it's something for breakfast. Nicki stopped over, and I haven't had time to eat, and I'm famished."

Moving to the small table, Sam put down the bag before replying, "In that case, you're in luck. I stopped at my Aunt's to pick up a loaf of bread for you, and she had just finished baking scones. She even threw in some clotted cream and strawberry jam. I just need to return her containers when they're empty."

Kate set the table before Sam could even finish talking and sat perched on her chair like a toddler waiting to be fed.

Laughing, Sam said, "I guess that means you would like me to make the tea, too."

Grabbing a still-warm scone. Kate replied, "If it's not too much trouble. I have my hands full at the moment. Shall I fix a scone for you, too?"

"Yes, please. Cream first and then jam."

Sitting the teapot on the table to steep, they tucked into the scones as they went over the plans for today.

"Nicki stopped over to tell us it appears that the victim died between the hours of 10 pm and 1 am three days before his remains had been discovered."

Nodding, Sam replied, "After we visit the Crown Prosecutors' offices, we need to revisit the family and find out where they were at the time of death. I have a team checking upriver to see if they can locate where the body went into the water. According to our local expert on the River Dart, it is likely that his body was dumped upstream and floated down with that heavy rain we had that week. Did Nicki mention anything to you about his stomach contents?"

"No, not that I recall."

Reaching into his pocket, Sam withdrew a copy of the autopsy report, "I made a copy for you to read, but according to this, it doesn't seem that Granville ate anything the last two days he was alive."

Scratching her head, Kate said, "That's interesting. Do you think he was abducted and held captive before being murdered?"

Nodding, Sam replied, "That's one theory that I feel is worth following up. We should know more if the team can locate where the body went in the river and expand a search from there for any likely places to keep someone prisoner without being detected."

The drive into town didn't take long, and they soon arrived at the Office of the Crown Prosecutor. Showing their identification papers at the front desk, the receptionist ushered them into the office of the Assistance Prosecutor.

Rising from his desk, the young man extended his hand and told them to take a seat. "I'm afraid that if you've come to speak with the Crown Prosecutor, he is currently on holiday in Scotland and left orders not to be disturbed. As you can imagine, his is a very stressful job, and this is the one break a year that he gets, so we never disturb him."

Kate was the first to respond, "Unfortunately, your boss is not in Scotland but at the morgue."

Looking confused, the young man blurted out, "Who's dead?"

To this, Sam replied, "Your boss."

Collapsing back in his chair and reaching for the glass of water on his desk, he asked, "What happened? Was it a shooting accident?"

Kate replied, "No, we're afraid not. Mr. Granville has been murdered.

"Oh dear God, his poor family," was all the shocked young man could mutter.

Kate continued, "What we have to ask you now is in the strictest confidence. We have the testimony from a knowledgeable person that Mr. Granville was romantically involved with an office staff member. We will need to speak with her to eliminate her from our inquiries."

"Ah, yes. I understand. Obviously, the young lady in question is no longer employed here, but I can get her details from personnel."

Fuming at the obvious sexist remark, Kate asked, "And why was she fired?"

"I thought that was obvious. We don't allow that type of behavior in this branch."

Kate stared the young man down, "If that is the case, why was Mr. Granville employed here?

Before he could answer, Kate turned to Sam, "Sounds like this young lady has a strong case for sexual discrimination. What do you think, Sam?"

Nodding, Sam replied through clenched teeth, "I couldn't agree more. Now, the young lady's details, please and hurry. We don't have time to sit around here all day. A murderer is walking free on the streets."

As they were about to step onto the elevator, a young woman raced after them and, quickly pushing the button to close the door, whispered, "I overheard what you said about Mr. Granville, and I think I have some information that might help you. Can we meet somewhere in private?"

Kate quickly responded, "Where and when?"

"I have my lunch break at noon. Can you meet me at the Old Crown pub on Fleet Street? It's a bit dodgy there, so no one from the office will likely see me talking to you."

Nodding, Kate confirmed the time and place as the elevator door opened, and they stepped out into the lobby.

"I wonder what all that is about? That young lady looked scared to death," said Sam.

Checking her wristwatch, Kate looked at Sam and said, "That's only forty minutes from now, so there's not enough time to go interview the young lady who was fired. What do you want to do in the meantime?"

"The office is only a five-minute walk from here. Let's stop in and see if the team has had any luck finding where the victim died."

Today was the first time that Kate had been to the station. It was a hive of activity, but everything stopped as all eyes turned to observe the new arrival in their midst.

"Team, I want to introduce you to Kate Lambert, Detective Chief Inspector with the MET. I know you all have heard me mention her, and I'm equally sure you have checked out her record of successful arrests. Kate will be taking the lead on the John-James Granville murder. Do we have any leads identifying the crime scene or where the body entered the river?"

A thin, balding detective looked down at his notes and replied, "We have two possibilities at the moment. Tire tracks lead to the river at two separate locations upstream. I am leaning toward being the most probable in an isolated area off a single-track road. There is an abandoned barn nearby, but we checked it out, and there didn't appear to be any sign of recent activity there. We're sending the forensic team out there to ensure we didn't miss anything."

"Any footprints leading from the tire tracks to the river?" asked Sam.

"Yes, we took impressions of the footprints and tire tracks at both locations. We are waiting for Dave Green to see if he can identify the possible vehicles involved."

"Murphy, have you checked into recent convictions that the Crown Prosecutor has made?"

The young officer looked up from his computer and replied, "Yes, sir. Today, I've read transcripts to see if the guilty parties made any verbal threats during the trial."

Kate walked over and stood behind the young officer before saying, "You may want to concentrate on his prosecution of Igor Smolenski or any other trials involving known affiliates of his."

"Alright then, Kate and I have several interviews to complete today, so we'll see you at 10 am sharp tomorrow for our next meeting. Anything comes up, ring my mobile," instructed Sam as the two detectives left for their meeting at the Old Crown pub.

They had just seated themselves at the table when the young woman from the Crown Prosecutors' office came through the door, eyes shifting around, checking that no one who knew her from work was there.

She approached the table and said, "Hi, I hate being so mysterious, but if anyone sees me talking to you, I might get in trouble, and I can't afford to lose this job."

"We completely understand. Can I get you something to eat and a drink?" asked Sam.

"A Diet Coke and a bag of crisps if you don't mind."

Looking toward Kate, Sam asked," Same for you?"

"Yes."

By the time Sam returned to the table, the two women had their heads close together, whispering, and he could tell by the expression on Kate's face that the young lady had said something alarming.

Setting the drinks down on the table, Sam asked, "What have I missed?"

The young woman looked pleadingly at Kate, "Do I have to tell it all over again?"

Reaching over and patting her hand, Kate said, "Not if you feel uncomfortable. I can give him the details after we've left. Did you happen to know Jennifer Collins?"

"Oh yes, everyone loved Jenny. Some people too much. She made me feel so welcome when I first started working there. I was so upset when they said she had turned in her resignation letter and left without a word. I wanted to thank her for being so nice to me, so I picked up a bouquet and went to her flat. She didn't answer the door, but the man in the next flat said she had been taken away in an ambulance the day before."

Sam cocked his head to one side, "Did he happen to know what was wrong with her?"

"No, and I knew Jenny didn't have any close family nearby, so I went to the hospital to see her, and when the first nurse told me she couldn't give me any information, I pretended to be her sister. The nurse said that Jenny had a termination, had hemorrhaged and lost a lot of blood before she phoned for help, so it was touch and go. I asked her how the hospital could have made that kind of mistake, and she said the termination had been done by someone unlicensed. Poor Jenny must have been so desperate. I visited her every day after work, and she finally admitted what had happened and warned me."

Sam asked, "What was her warning?"

She said, "Stay clear of Mr. Granville. Never be alone in his company. She said he had taken advantage of her and had gotten her pregnant. Then when she told him, he sent her to this butcher, and now poor Jenny will never be able to have children."

"Did Granville ever try to compromise you?" asked Sam.

Kate looked into Sam's eyes before saying, "We've already discussed that, so I'll fill you in later. We better let this young lady enjoy the rest of her lunch hour."

After taking her name and contact details and giving her their cards, the two detectives walked out of the pub into the cloudy and rainy afternoon.

"At least the weather matches my mood after that conversation. Somehow, I think whoever murdered that disgusting, vile predator did a lot of young women a service," said Kate.

Chapter 10

Sam avoided eye contact with Kate for the rest of the drive to Jennifer Collins' flat on the other side of town. Whatever the young girl had told her about her abuse at the hands of Granville must have been horrific to upset a veteran detective the way it had. It was a conversation best left for later, he wisely decided.

Arriving at the address, Kate turned to Sam, "Listen, I'm not pulling rank or trying to be sexist, but I think Ms. Collins might feel very uncomfortable discussing her experiences in front of a man. If it is alright with you, I will explain to her that you are the local detective in charge and ask her if she objects to your presence while being questioned."

Holding his hands up in surrender, Sam replied, "I have no objection whatsoever. I have two sisters, and I know certain discussions are off-limits. I'm more than happy to wait in the car unless she agrees to meet me."

Before Kate could even knock on the door to the flat, a painfully thin, young blonde opened it. Ushering Kate into the flat, she said, "Megan called and said she had spoken to you, so I expected you."

Leading Kate into the small lounge, she pointed to a chair before continuing, "Megan said she had told you what Granville did to me, but there's more to the story. I had a good position as a law clerk at the office, and John made me believe he was mentoring me. I was too naive to realize that John was grooming me instead. It started with a casual brushing against me as he passed by, then escalated over months. Then one evening, when we were alone in the office, he made his move. I told him to stop and that I would report him to the police, but he just laughed and asked me which of us I thought the police would believe. It only took that one time, and when I missed my period, I realized that I was pregnant. He told me not to say anything if I wanted to keep my job. He said he knew a good doctor who owed him a favor. His so-called good doctor botched it, and I ended up in the hospital, and you know the rest of the story," she sobbed.

Kate placed a comforting hand on the young girl's arm, "I assume that Megan told you that your former boss is dead," said Kate.

"Yes, she did, and I can't say I'm sorry."

Kate nodded, "I can sympathize with your feelings on that; unfortunately, it is our job to interview anyone who may have a motive to wish him dead, and unfortunately, that's what brings us here. My partner is waiting in the car. Would it be alright for him to come in now that we have discussed what happened to you? He'll just ask for your movements around the time of the crime."

Nodding her head, Jenny acknowledged that it was okay, and Kate went to the door and motioned for Sam to join them.

"Jenny, this is Detective Sam Adams. He is your local detective working on the case. If you can provide him with the details of your movements during the times in question, I'll fix you a cup of tea."

Jenny smiled, "Thanks, you'll find the tea bags in the cupboard above the cooker, and I take milk and sugar."

The interview was over by the time Kate returned from the kitchen with Jenny's cup of tea. As the two detectives walked to the door, Kate turned to Jenny and handed her card to the young victim, saying, "If you ever need to talk or would like to be referred to a counselor, that's my mobile number. You can call me anytime."

Jenny looked at the card and mumbled, "Thank you. You have both been very kind. You'll forgive me if I say that whoever rid the world of him deserves a medal."

Once they were in the car, Kate looked at Sam and said, "You know, I couldn't blame her if she had something to do with Granville's death."

"I seriously doubt that she did. I still need to have them checked out, but she seems to have pretty solid alibis for the times in question. Plus, after what Granville did to her, she would likely have cut off some other organ and not bother with his head and hands," replied Sam.

"We agree on that point," chuckled Kate before continuing, "I think whoever murdered Granville didn't want him identified right away and didn't know him well enough to know about the rod in his leg."

"Or they knew about the rod and weren't aware of the manufacturer's numbering."

Kate conceded, "Point well taken. We know the family must have been aware of the injury, but they might not have been aware of the numbering, so we still need to check their movements."

Looking at her watch, Kate asked, "Is this something we can do tomorrow? It's almost 5 pm, and I haven't eaten since those scones this morning."

"No problem at all. I need to stop at the shops before they close, or I'll have no dinner tonight."

Kate thought about the two large lamb chops she had bought two days ago and asked, "Do you eat lamb?"

"Of course. Why?"

"I have two nice-sized chops in the refrigerator that need cooking tonight, or they'll go off, and I can only eat one. So, if you'd like to stay for dinner, you're welcome."

"Only if you let me do the washing up!"

"It's a deal. I don't mind cooking, but I loathe the clean-up."

Dinner that evening was a quiet affair with no discussion of the case as both detectives enjoyed their first proper meal of the day.

Pushing back from the table, Sam patted his stomach, "That was a delicious meal, Detective Chief Inspector. Without a doubt, the best meal that I've had since moving down here."

Raising her eyebrows, Kate asked, "Wait, I thought you were born and raised around here."

Sam said, "No, I grew up in Hampshire, but I always spent the summers here with my Aunt. I loved the beaches and the lush countryside, so I moved here permanently after completing school."

"Is your family still in Hampshire?"

"Only one of my sisters. She married a footballer and lives in a house on the Basingstoke canal outside Fleet. One sister is up in Berkshire, and the other stayed with mum until she passed and then moved to New Zealand."

"I know Fleet very well. I used to catch the train there to go to London when first working for the MET. My family home was in Church Crookham, and I stayed with mum and dad until they passed. After that, I sold up and bought a small flat in the City close to work."

Sam smiled, "Lovely area, Fleet. Lots of really great restaurants and a pub on almost every corner. Everything a bachelor might want."

Kate couldn't help but notice that Sam's smile had suddenly disappeared, and his mood darkened. She wondered what had happened in his past to cause this shift in attitude.

"Care to talk about what's just upset you?" asked Kate.

"It's no secret, I guess, and I'm amazed that Nicki hasn't mentioned it already. I was due to be married, but on the day, Emily, the bride-to-be, never turned up at the church. When I went to her apartment, she had cleared out. I spoke to the landlady, and she told me that Emily told her that she was going to the States to reconcile with her husband. Can you believe it? I didn't have a clue that she was married and me a detective."

"That's horrible! No, Nicki never mentioned anything other than to say you were handsome and unattached. How long did you and Emily know each other?"

"Almost a year. We bumped into each other at the Saturday market and got to chatting. You know how it goes. I invited her to join me for a coffee at Starbucks, and she accepted. The next week, we met up at the market again, and it grew from there. The worse bit was I found out later that Emily wasn't even her real name. Everything about her was a lie, and I was too blinded to notice."

Kate couldn't help but remember her loss and anguish, but it was still too raw to share with her new partner. After a few minutes of painful silence, Kate pushed back from the table and gathered up the dishes.

Throwing a pair of Marigolds at him, she smiled and said, "I believe you volunteered to do the washing up."

Sam hadn't been gone five minutes when Nicki knocked on their adjoining door, "Can I come in?"

Unlocking the door, Nicki bounced into the room, beaming, "Do I sense a romance blooming?"

Shaking her head, Kate said," Uh...no. Neither of us had eaten, and since I had two chops that needed cooking, I invited him to stay. Besides, he offered to wash up, and I hate that part of the job, and while we are talking, why didn't you tell me about his almost marriage?"

"Sorry, Kate. I figured that you would eventually hear it from someone else. I'm not one to gossip, " said Nicki as her eyes clouded.

Quickly picking up on Nicki's mood change, Kate gently asked, "Have you been the victim of nasty gossip, too?"

"Of course, haven't you? Any woman doing what some people view as a man's job has to put up with it."

The sound of a phone ringing from next door had Nicki up on her feet and racing to her cottage.

After she left, Kate fixed a cup of tea, sat down staring out the window into the dark, and murmured, "I will almost bet money that Nicki has something in her past that she'd much rather not have anyone knowing about."

Chapter 11

The next day, Sam had arranged for them to interview Granville's family and their employees in the afternoon. The morning briefing would undoubtedly swallow up most of the morning. The incident room was a beehive of activity as the team gathered in front of a large map tacked to the notice board.

"Sir, we have some information back from Dave Green regarding the tire tracks. They are, as we suspected, made by a compact car. His best guess would be a Mini or something of a similar size. The tread appeared fairly new too. As for the footprints, those are a bit harder to judge. The tracks were made by someone wearing Wellies, so their shoe size could be smaller than the actual footprint."

Sam frowned, "So let me get this straight, we are looking for a compact car, possibly a Mini, with relatively new tires and someone, male or female, with undetermined shoe size. Well, that's half of the population of Devon. Come on, team, we need more to go on!"

Going into his office and slamming the door, a frustrated Sam turned to Kate, "Any ideas?"

"If the team is somewhat certain that these two areas are probable sites for the victim entering the river, it might be worthwhile to have a team of divers go in the river there."

"I'm not following you," replied Sam leaning forward in his chair.

Leaning across the desk towards him, she said, "If I were dumping a body in the river that I had just dismembered, I would drop the saw in with him."

Jumping up from his chair, Sam flung open the office door and called, "Jim, get a team of divers over to the river at those two locations and have them look for anything the perpetrator could use to dismember the victim."

Dropping back down in his chair, Sam let out a long sigh, looked over to Kate, and said, "Thanks for that. Now, do you understand why I asked your boss to assign you to this case? I'm sorry if it messed up your plans for early retirement, but this is the first crime of this nature that I've covered, and I'm not too proud to take advice from a more experienced senior officer."

From twenty years of experience on the force, Kate recognized that it took a lot for Sam to admit that he needed her help. It made him a better officer and a better man in her eyes.

The rest of the morning flew by without any further developments in the case, and it was soon time for a quick lunch before they made the drive to Millstone Manor.

Over lunch in the building cafeteria, Sam apologized again for upsetting Kate's retirement plans and asked, "How were you planning on filling your hours during retirement?

"I have always wanted to write mysteries, and with my background, I felt I might have a shot at making a good job of it."

Nodding as he bit into his ham and cheese sandwich, Sam swallowed and said, "I bet you'll be great at it. Let me know if you need anyone to edit them for you."

"Why do you know a good editor who works cheap?" asked Kate as she pushed the rather unappetizing salad around on her plate. She would much rather have had a large plate of chips and vinegar, but her waistline was unforgiving.

"How about for free?"

Kate smirked, "Yeah, where are you going to find a free, good editor?"

Sitting back in his seat, he thumbed himself, saying, "You're looking at him. My degree at Uni was in English, and my first job was a short stint as an editor with one of the larger publishing houses in London."

Kate looked astonished, "I never took you for the literary type. Well done, you."

With that settled, they finished their lunches and headed for the car to drive to the Manor. As they maneuvered down the narrow hedgerow-lined lanes, Kate spoke first, "I vote that we interview the young gardener first and ask him about the affair he's been carrying on with the lady of the house."

Chuckling, Sam replied, "I agree. I can imagine that he will be shocked to know that his alleged, discreet affair with his employer is now a matter of public knowledge."

Laughing aloud, "No more than the seemingly prim and proper Mrs. Granville. It seems that both she and her husband were not above seeking out younger lovers."

"We'll have to tread lightly. We only have Mrs. Robert's testimony to go on, and it all could be a matter of sour grapes. She did seem genuinely fond of Mr. Granville, and perhaps there are bad feelings between the two women," replied Sam.

Shading her eyes from the sun as it filtered through the giant oak trees approaching the Manor, Cat said, "I tend to believe the housekeeper. I don't think that much goes on at that house that she doesn't know. We already know from experience that she is quite adept at listening at doors."

Finding the gardener was much easier than they had anticipated. As they pulled onto the gravel drive, they were just in time to see him enter the substantial greenhouse at the side of the stately home.

"Ah…looks like we arrived at the perfect time," stated Sam as he exited the car and strode toward the Victorian-styled greenhouse.

It was a sunny and warm day, and the heat and humidity within the building had Kate slipping off her jacket as they approached the young gardener, who had by now stripped off his t-shirt and stood bare-chested watering seedlings.

Checking out the gardener, Kate whispered to Sam, "I can see the attraction."

Sam's mouth flew open, but nothing came out as he approached the young man and produced his warrant card.

Pointing to Kate, he announced, "This is Detective Chief Inspector Kate Lambert of the MET, and I am Detective Sam Adams with the Devon Constabulary. Your name, sir?"

Grabbing his t-shirt and pulling it back over his head, he replied, "Jeff Smith. Is there something I can do for you?"

Not to mince words, Kate jumped right in, "How long has your affair with Mrs. Granville been going on?"

Dropping his long body into the closest chair, he stuttered his answer, "Did she tell you?"

Continuing the attack, Kate responded, "No, she did not, but are you aware that your affair has become public knowledge, and this might implement you in the murder of her husband?"

"What!" he shouted as he jumped up wide-eyed, knocking over his chair.

The young man took on the appearance of a wild animal caught in a trap and exclaimed, "He knew all about it and even paid me to keep the old lady happy."

Taking Kate by surprise by his answer, Sam repeated what the gardener had said, "You're telling us that Mr. Granville paid you extra to sleep with his wife?"

The young man calmed down a little, "Well, that and take care of the gardens."

Finally composed, Kate asked, "Where did these assignations occur?"

Cocking his head to the side, he asked, "Assignations?"

Losing patience, Sam replied, "Look, don't be thick. Where were you having sex with Mrs. Granville."

A smile played briefly across the young gardener's face before he answered, "Mostly in the woods. She liked doing it outside and sometimes in the stables or barn if the weather was wet, except she always had to be on top in there because she said the straw bothered her bottom."

"OK, too much information. We need to know where you were the weekend beginning June 15th."

Scratching his head for a moment, he finally smiled and said, "I was at the Agricultural Show, down Exeter way. I was there all weekend. I even have receipts for the plants I bought for the Manor."

Before leaving the greenhouse, Sam got Smith's details and advised him not to leave the area while the investigation was ongoing.

As they walked across the drive to the house, Sam looked at Kate and smirked, "Well, that was enlightening."

Eliza Roberts answered the door at the sound of their first knock, "The Missus is in the library. She's expecting you if you'll follow me."

Mrs. Granville was standing with her back turned, gazing out the window as they entered the room.

She said, "I see you've been admiring my greenhouse," turning to greet them. "It's a reproduction of the actual Victorian conservatory that stood on that very spot in its day."

"No. We were interviewing your gardener, Mr. Smith, regarding your ongoing extra-marital affair," replied Kate.

"Oh, that?" remarked the new widow with a flourish of her hands.

"Yes, that Mrs. Granville," retorted Kate.

"If you will excuse me for a minute. Mrs. Roberts, I know you're listening at the door. Would you be good enough to bring the nice detectives and me some tea and biscuits? Now, what can I tell you about my outrageous behavior that my good housekeeper has not?"

Kate began to soften a bit toward the woman. At least the widow had chutzpah and asked, "Based on what you both have admitted, would you care to tell us why we shouldn't be investigating either you or your lover in the death of your husband?"

Smiling, she replied, "I'm afraid it would be quite a few of my previous lovers over the years who you might have to add to your suspect list. My husband rewarded them very well to keep me busy and out of his sordid business. There was a time when I would have divorced him and taken the twins and left, but after my first affair, he began threatening me. Although I knew about all his disgusting relationships with girls younger than the twins, I had no real proof, and none of those girls would have volunteered to tell their stories in an open courtroom. He used the power of his position to get away with it with them and me. And before you ask, I didn't kill my husband or have anything to do with his murder, although I must confess that I wished him dead."

The door swung open as Mrs. Roberts entered the room with the tea. Looking directly at her, Mrs. Granville said, "Eliza, maybe now would be a good time for you to tell the kind detectives why my husband has kept you close to him and taken such good care of you all these years."

Never changing her expression, Mrs. Roberts turned her back and said, "I ain't got nothing to tell," and left the room.

Pouring Kate and Sam a cup of tea, Mrs. Granville began the story of an unwed mother whose son rose to the position of Crown Prosecutor and the owner of a fine Manor House.

Kate couldn't help but be shocked, "Are you telling us that Eliza Roberts is your husband's mother, and he has kept her on here working as his housekeeper and treated her like nothing more than paid help?"

"That is what I'm telling you. To be quite honest, I wouldn't be surprised if Eliza killed John. The way he treated her after all her sacrifices to get him educated. If it weren't for her taking any job, John would never have attained his position. He was a selfish egomaniac and couldn't bear the thought of anyone knowing who his birth mother was. Yet, she still worshipped the ground he walked on. That was until lately. I don't know what changed, but something did. If I were you, I would think of adding Eliza to your list of suspects."

After finishing their tea, they asked Mrs. Granville about her movements the weekend her husband went missing. She advised them that her sister and two sons had spent the entire weekend with her at the Manor, not leaving until Monday morning when she took them to the train station. She readily furnished them with her sister's details and informed them that the twins were at Uni but would be home on the weekend if they could wait to speak further with them until then.

"There is one more thing we need to clear up," stated Kate.

Looking straight at Kate, Mrs. Granville responded, "Ask me anything. I want this tragedy cleared up for no other reason but the twins' sake. My husband wasn't much of a father, but he was still their father."

78

"I understand. During the autopsy, the coroner discovered he had a rod in his leg indicative of a broken femur at some point during your marriage. Can you give us any details on how the injury occurred?"

Mrs. Granville started laughing, much to their surprise, before saying, "I'm sorry, but it's rather a funny story."

Sam stared as he replied, "I can't think of anything funny about a broken femur. Care to explain?"

"Well, it happened on one of my husband's little work trips. His work called me to tell me that he had phoned and there had been a skiing accident and John would be delayed returning to work. Of course, being a fairly new bride, I was alarmed and caught the first flight to the hospital in Austria and raced to his bedside. When I arrived at the hospital, the nurse on duty informed me that I would have to wait to go to his room because his wife was with him. Well, of course, I didn't, and as soon as she turned her back, I headed down the hall to his room. I was just in time to witness his so-called wife giving him a rather intimate massage, if you get my meaning. It was the first time I'd caught him in the act, and I'm afraid I behaved badly. I threw the slut out of the room after punching her in the eye."

Trying to hide the smile on his lips as he pictured the scene, Sam nodded and said, "Thank you very much for clearing that up."

After agreeing to call on the family that coming weekend, Kate and Sam took their leave. As they started the car to leave, Kate observed, "We're being watched. It looks like the victim's mother is eager for us to leave. I'd love to be a fly on the wall to hear what happens between mother and daughter-in-law after we drive away."

Shaking his head, Sam said, "The more I hear about Granville, the more I wonder how he didn't end up in the river a lot sooner than he did."

Kate laughed, "It's a wonder our demure widow didn't smother him with his pillow right there in the hospital!"

Becoming serious again, Kate said, "We'll have to speak to his mother again and try to find out what happened recently to cause friction between them. That being said, I can't picture a mother, especially one as frail as she dismembering a body and having the strength to get it into the river. Even if she did, how would she have gotten the body there? When I ran a check on her, it doesn't appear that she even has a driver's license."

Sam rolled his eyes, "Now, Kate, just because a person doesn't have a license, it doesn't mean that they can't drive."

Raising her eyebrows, Kate just replied, "True, but I'd still put her way down at the bottom of the list of suspects."

It had been a long day, and Sam dropped Kate off at her cottage just as Nicki pulled into her drive. Waving to Sam as he drove off, Nicki yelled, "Care for a glass of wine?"

"Sure. I'll be right over," replied Kate as she closed her cottage door and then freshened up before tapping on Nicki's door.

"Come on in! It's unlocked."

Nicki was uncorking the wine and pouring two good-sized portions as Kate dropped down in the nearest chair.

"Tough day, huh?" asked Nicki.

"Let's just say it was very revealing and somewhat shocking."

"Do tell!" exclaimed Nicki as she passed Kate a glass and sat opposite her.

Before continuing, Kate said, taking a long sip, "You know, we both knew that Granville was a bastard of the first class, but he took it to another level entirely."

"Well, I told you that I had heard things about him in the past but wrote it off to jealousy of his position or the work of people for whom he had gotten convictions," said Nicki with a shrug of her shoulders.

Kate stared into her wine glass, "I might as well tell you because you'll hear it anyway once the story gets out."

Nicki said, sitting on the edge of her chair, "What?"

"Well, have you ever met Eliza Roberts?"

Slowly shaking her head, Nicki stared down at the floor, "No, I don't think so."

"Well, she's the housekeeper at Millstone Manor, and today we discovered that she is John Granville's mother."

Staring back at Kate with a shocked expression, Nicki exclaimed, "That can't be."

"Why not? I guess it was a way to keep his mother close without everyone knowing she was his mother and that he was a bastard. From what her daughter-in-law tells us, she doted on him until recently, when something changed, and her attitude changed dramatically. Sam and I will talk with her again tomorrow evening after she gets off work to see if she will tell us anything."

Swishing the wine around in her glass, Nicki asked, "Does this wine taste alright?"

"Yes, why?" asked Kate.

"I suddenly feel very nauseous. I think I better lay down. I'm probably overtired and shouldn't have had this wine on an empty stomach. Please excuse me."

As Kate was leaving, she called over her shoulder, "Call me or knock at the door if you need anything. Hope you feel better!"

Chapter 12

The next day was the usual rounds with the team at the incident room. Due to a training mission, the divers weren't available until the following day, so there was nothing to report on the river search.

The database checks on Granville's court cases revealed no obvious threats against him, but the young officer expanded his search into older proceedings.

Kate was becoming frustrated that no breaks in the case had emerged five days into the investigation.

"How about we go out and see for ourselves these two potential dump sites for the victim? I want to do a thorough foot search of the area for any out-of-the-way buildings used in the commission of the crime."

"I don't know what you expect to find that the forensics team failed to find, but since there's nothing to be done here, we might as well," replied Sam.

"Another couple sets of eyes can't hurt, and we'll be in the direction of Mrs. Roberts's cottage, then we can call in there on the way home."

"Sounds like a good plan, but first, let's grab some sandwiches and drinks for lunch. If we are going to walk along the river, we might as well have a picnic with us," replied Sam as he grabbed his car keys and headed for the door.

Laughing out loud, Kate called after him, "Typical bloke. Always thinking about your stomach."

After stopping at Tesco and picking up a few ready-made sandwiches, crisps, and drinks, they made their way to the first place indicated on the map furnished by the team.

"It sure is isolated enough. I wouldn't have known this track leading to the river existed unless I was very familiar with the area," said Sam as he guided his car over the many ruts in the road.

There was evidence of fly-tipping to the left of where the road ended. Someone had recently dumped old tires and garden waste in a huge pile, despite signs everywhere prohibiting it. The swarm of flies buzzing around the stack and the odor wafting up from it led Kate to believe the dump included food waste.

Turning up her nose at the smell, Kate said, "No picnic here."

"I agree. I know of a better place a little farther on," replied Sam.

Parking as far away from the fly-tip as possible, they exited the car and got their Wellies from the trunk. As they walked closer to the river, they could see where forensics had poured the mixture into the tire tracks to make the impressions. Since his team had combed over the area, there were footprints of every size and shape now. Turning away from the river, they walked in a broad circular arc. Other than the typical trash, there wasn't anything they thought could have been related to the abduction and murder, so they moved on to site two.

Driving down the narrow road, Kate kept her eye out for any buildings that might have suited the abductor's requirements. They had just rounded a bend when Sam pulled the car over and stopped.

"I thought that this would be a good place to picnic. If we walk through that small wooded area that runs along the river, we'll find a large boulder we can sit on to eat. I used to come here berry picking with my Aunt, and I remember it well."

Kate smiled as she pictured a young barefooted Sam trotting along behind his dotting aunt and eating as many berries as he picked.

"Sounds lovely," said Kate as she grabbed the bag containing their lunch and followed Sam through the woods.

They had just finished eating lunch when Sam's mobile went off.

"Adams. What time did she call? Alright, we aren't far from there. Call her back and tell her we'll be with her shortly."

Disconnecting the call, Sam turned to Kate, "That was the office. Mrs. Granville called and seemed very troubled and asked that we come to her home."

Shoving the last bit of her sandwich in her mouth, Kate replied, "We better get over there then. It must be important to upset her. That woman has nerves of steel."

Fifteen minutes later, they arrived at Millhouse Manor to find Mrs. Granville standing at the open front door, wringing her hands.

Rushing up to the car, she exclaimed, "I'm glad you came so quickly. I'm so terribly worried."

Getting out of the car, Kate put her arm around the older woman's shoulder, "Calm down now, and tell us what's happened."

"It's Eliza. We had a terrible argument last night after you left. She was upset that I told you that she was John's mother. You understand we argue all the time, but this is the first time she hasn't shown up for work in the morning. I waited until noon, just thinking she was trying to teach me a lesson and would be here later but when she didn't come, I phoned and got no answer. I'm very fond of the old dear, despite what you might think, and I'm afraid she might have done something to hurt herself."

Sam started the car up as Kate tried to direct Mrs. Granville into the house, but she pulled away and climbed into the back seat, shouting, "I'm going with you!"

Gravel flew as Sam gunned the engine and tore down the drive towards Oakview Cottage. There was no sign of life when they parked out front: no lights and no sign of activity. As Sam started to knock on the door, he noticed that it was already slightly ajar and quickly motioned for Kate to follow him.

"Stay in the car, Mrs. Granville," ordered Kate as she disappeared into the cottage.

Kate slowly climbed the stairs while Sam checked the rooms downstairs.

"Up here, Sam!" Kate called as she dialed 999.

Mrs. Roberts was lying in a bath of red water, with her wrists slashed. It was evident from the older woman's pallor and blood loss that she was dead, but Kate still put her fingers to the woman's neck for confirmation.

Turning as Sam entered the room, she said, "Better give Nicki a call. We're going to need her. I'll stay with Mrs. Roberts and wait for the emergency services while you take Mrs. Granville home and get that gardener to sit with her until we get back there."

As Kate waited, she pulled up a chair from the bedroom and sat observing the body. It was evident that she had cut her wrists and bled out, but where was the razor? An empty bottle of what was labeled a sleeping potion sat open on the small table beside an empty wine glass. Leaning in closely, Kate noticed slight bruising on Eliza's face and wondered if Eliza and her daughter-in-law had thrown around more than words last night. Something didn't feel right, but Nicki would be able to rule out foul play once she got the victim back to the morgue. Now all Kate could do was wait.

Chapter 13

After arriving and leaving the ambulance attendants to take Mrs. Roberts to the morgue, Kate and Sam drove back to Millstone Manor to speak with Mrs. Granville. The front door was ajar, and after calling out, they entered the library to find Mrs. Granville sitting and staring out the window.

"She's killed herself, hasn't she? And it's all my fault!" she sobbed.

"It would appear that she has, but we'll have to await the findings from the coroner. If she decided to end her own life, that was her decision and hers alone. If it does turn out to be suicide, you mustn't blame yourself. I don't have children, but they say that a child's loss is something many parents don't recover from," gently replied Kate.

Nodding, Sam added, "Unfortunately, that's very true. The sudden death of her son may well have been enough to tip her over the edge. From what you have told us, she spent her whole life looking out for her son and protecting him."

Still sobbing into her handkerchief, the widow moaned, "I just wish I knew what he had done that made her turn on him at the end. It must have been something horrific for her not to be able to forgive him. Eliza hardly spoke to John during the last few weeks of his life. And when she did, it wasn't pleasant. I tried asking her what was causing the friction between them, but she told me to mind my own business."

"We wondered about that after you told us that your husband was Eliza's son. When we first interviewed her, she was more than happy to condemn John's behavior and even told us where to go to ask about one of his victims," said Sam

"My God! Whatever John did must have been horrific to turn her love to hate. You don't suppose she did kill him and felt so guilt-ridden that she decided to end her own life?"

"That's one theory that we'll be exploring," replied Kate as questions about Mrs. Robert's death scene swirled around in her mind.

After comforting Mrs. Granville, the two detectives started to leave. As Kate approached the door, she turned and asked, "When you and your mother-in-law argued last night, did things get physical?"

"No, of course not! I could never harm Eliza. Despite appearances, she was my only real friend in this god-forsaken house."

As soon as they reached the car, Kate turned to Sam, "I need to discover what caused Eliza to fall out with her son. We must go back and search her cottage from top to bottom."

"Why did you ask Mrs. Granville if their argument became physical?"

"I noticed a slight discoloration on Eliza's cheek, but it might be nothing. She might have done it herself before or after getting in the bath. From the looks of it, she seemed to have been drinking heavily that morning."

Just nodding, Sam drove out the drive and headed in the direction of Oakview Cottage.

As they pulled up to the cottage, they could just make out the taillights of the ambulance carrying Mrs. Roberts' remains to the morgue. Climbing the stairs, Kate found the bathroom just as she had left it. The only difference was the blood-stained water on the floor left from where the attendants had lifted the deceased from the tub. The tub was still filled with bloody water. Kate grabbed the metal chain and pulled the plug, watching the water slowly drain. There was no sign of a razor or anything else that could have caused the slash marks on the deceased wrists. Kate was just getting up from crawling around on hands and knees, looking for anything that could have caused the wounds, when Sam walked up behind her, "What in the world are you doing?"

"Something doesn't make sense. If you are sitting in a bath getting ready to end your life, where would you likely put the razor or whatever else you use?"

"Looking around the small bathroom, Sam's eyes alighted on the wastebasket. Reaching his gloved hand inside, he withdrew a shiny straight razor blade, "Is this what you are looking for?"

Shaking her head, Kate replied," I don't think it is likely that Mrs. Roberts slashed her wrists and then got out of the tub to throw the razor in the wastebasket. Do you? Besides, she would have left wet tracks on the floor, and the tile was perfectly dry when I found her."

"I see your point, but let's just wait for Nicki's autopsy and the forensics report. In the meantime, I think I found something that explains why Eliza was so upset with her son," said Sam as he passed Kate a small piece of notepaper. It was type-written and only contained eight words... *I didn't know she was your sister's child.*

Leaning over her shoulder as she read, Sam asked, "What do you make of that?"

"I'd say that it appears Granville's philandering struck a little too close to home for his mother's liking."

"Sure sounds like it to me, too," replied Sam, taking the note from Kate and slipping it into an evidence bag.

Using his gloved hand, Sam picked up the empty wine glass and wine bottle and slipped each into separate bags, "Might as well get these back to the lab and check for fingerprints. Alright, let's get back to the station and see if we can track down Mrs. Roberts' sister and that daughter of hers," said Sam.

While Sam was driving, Kate quickly called Mrs. Granville to ask if she might know Eliza's sister's name.

After tearfully listening, Mrs. Granville said, "Eliza didn't have a sister, or at least she never mentioned having one, but that may have been down to her parents throwing her out in the streets and disowning her when she got pregnant. To be honest, I don't know if Roberts was even her birth name or where the name Granville came from."

"Well, thank you, Mrs. Granville. We'll be in touch," sighed Kate disconnecting the call.

"What's with that big sigh?" asked Sam as he glanced at Kate's troubled face.

"Oh, this case just gets more and more complex. Just when we think that we have a lead, it just gets more convoluted. Mrs. Granville never heard Eliza speak of a sister, and she doesn't even know if Roberts was Eliza's birth name or if Granville was her husband's birth name."

"Oh great!" swore Sam as he banged his palms against the steering wheel.

The rest of the journey into town was made in dead silence as both detectives pondered their next move.

Chapter 14

As soon as they arrived at the incident room, a long-haired, young detective, whom Sam introduced as Bob Collins, approached them.

"We reviewed the cameras' tapes at the train station, and Granville boarded the 9:25 to London. The MET picked him up on the cameras from there, and you'll never guess!"

Clearly frustrated, Sam snapped, "We don't have time to play guessing games! Where did he go from there?"

Blushing at the rebuke, the young detective replied, "That's the funny bit. He turned around and caught the very next train back here. When he returned, we picked him up again at the station but lost him when he headed off into a wooded area outside the camera's range."

"That is strange. Thanks for following up on that, Bob," replied a much calmer Sam.

"Any word on whether the divers found anything in the river?"

This time, Bob quickly answered, "Yes, they located what they described as a large blade at the second site, have bagged it, and will drop it off at forensics."

Nodding toward Kate, Sam said, "Right again about the murder weapon dump. What's the odds that the murderer left any prints?"

Shaking her head, "Probably zero."

Entering his office and shutting the door, he asked Kate, "Any theories of why Granville would bother to ride the train to London and then immediately turn around and return without even leaving the station?"

Leaning back in her chair, Kate surmised, "I can think of several. First, have Bob and his contact at the MET go back and review those tapes. See if Granville interacted with anyone during his time at the station. Have them check out petite, blonde females taking the train back to Devon. Perhaps he was meeting a woman there, and their plans changed. Second, we don't have the victim's phone, but we can get his phone number and have the company furnish any records of outgoing and incoming numbers. Perhaps whomever he was meeting phoned him with a change of plans. Finally, have some of the men speak to the guards on the train and see if they noticed him. If they did, and something seemed wrong, they might have noticed. If Bob and his counterpart at the MET don't pick up on anything unusual, I want to review them myself. Someone like Granville doesn't just take the train to London and come straight back unless he is up to something."

"Excellent theories, and that's why you get paid the big bucks," quipped a smiling Sam.

"Big bucks, my arse," was Kate's only reply as she strode out of Sam's office in search of a cup of strong coffee.

Returning with two large coffees from the neighbouring Starbucks, Kate deposited one in front of Sam, "Cream and two sugars."

"Ah, you remembered?" grinned Sam.

"I damn well should. If my calculations are right, this is the third time I've had to pick up and pay for your coffee."

"Whoa! Stop right there. For one, I didn't ask you to get me a coffee, and second, if I had, I would have offered to pay for yours and mine."

"Chauvinist!"

"Oh, for the love of God. A guy just can't win with you, can he?" replied Sam as he tried to push his coffee back over in front of Kate.

Laughing, Kate pushed the coffee back, "I'm only teasing you. Can't you take a joke? I was just trying to lighten the mood."

Sam reached out and grabbed the coffee before muttering, "Thanks, I'll get the next ones."

Leaning forward with her elbows on Sam's desk, Kate asked. "When do you anticipate that Nicki might finish that autopsy on Eliza?"

"Hopefully, later today. I get the impression that Nicki is treating it as a cut-and-dried suicide."

Wrinkling her forehead, Kate murmured, "I'm not so sure of that. Certain things just don't make sense to me."

Not eager to add another murder investigation to the middle of the current one, Sam curtly replied, "I'm sure Nicki knows her job, so let's just leave it to the expert, shall we?"

Kate abruptly got up from her chair and made to leave Sam's office.

"Where are you going?"

"Since you don't value my opinions regarding Mrs. Robert's suspicious death, I'm off to research the one case I'm assigned. "

Sam called after her, following her out his office door, "Just because we don't agree on everything doesn't mean you have to get your knickers in a twist."

Turning on him, Kate retorted, "Very professional, Detective Adams," before storming out of the incident room.

All eyes in the incident room turned to stare at Sam as he strode back into his office, slamming the door.

Kate was fuming as she made her way towards High Street. Remembering that she had left her coffee on Sam's desk, she made for the nearest tea room. After ordering a pot of tea, she pulled her mobile out and placed a call to Commander Morgan.

Answering on the first ring, he said, "Lambert, Good to hear from you. How's it going down there?"

"Not as quickly as I'd have liked," she grumbled.

"Why? What's going on?"

"It's Detective Adams. I'm not sure I can continue working on this case with him."

"You'll have to give me more details before I can remove you from the case and have another officer assigned. What's the young detective done?"

"It's more what he hasn't done. We've had another suspicious death directly related to the Granville murder."

"Related?"

"Yes, Sir. In more ways than one. The victim of an alleged suicide was Granville's birth mother, who strangely enough had been working as his housekeeper."

"Alleged suicide, huh?"

"Yes, Sir. We discovered Mrs. Roberts in the bath with her wrists cut, but the razor she allegedly used was across the room in the wastebasket."

"I see. Maybe the deceased cut her wrists before she got in the bath or got up from the bath and threw the razor away."

"Yeah, that was Adam's theory, except when I discovered the body, the floor was perfectly dry, and there wasn't a trace of blood on the floor."

"OK. I'm getting the picture now. And Adams is unwilling to listen to your concerns?"

"Yeah, told me to leave it to their expert, Nicki Hopwood, the coroner."

"OK, any reason you think the coroner isn't up to the job?"

"I think Nicki is just writing it off as the suicide of a grieving mother. To be perfectly honest, I don't think they get many murders here."

"Well, have you confronted this Nicki with your concerns?"

"That's a little delicate, Sir. The coroner is my landlady, lives in the adjoining cottage, and is the only friend I've made here."

"Oh, I see. I have a coordination briefing with Adams this afternoon and will address the issues. He's bound to bring up Granville's mother's death, and when he gives me the details, I will express my concerns about the suicide verdict. That should get him off your ass. Don't forget, you outrank him and are the lead, in this case, so don't let him push you around."

"Yes, Sir. Thanks, speak to you soon."

Feeling bolstered by her boss's words, Kate poured herself another cup of tea from the small pot and looked out onto the street. She was just in time to see Sam slowly walking up the road, looking in every window. She tapped on the window as he approached the tea shop to let him know she was there.

Dropping down into the only vacant chair at the small table, he said, "Sorry to bother you on your tea break, but we've just received some information on Eliza Robert's sister that I thought might interest you."

Just nodding for him to continue, Kate drank her tea and stared out the window.

"You remember asking one of the team to check cases involving Igor Smolenski or any of his affiliates?"

At the mention of Smolenski's name, Kate turned to stare at Sam, "What's the team uncovered?"

"It appears that Eliza's younger sister was involved in a brief affair with Smolenski, which resulted in the birth of a daughter. The mother has since died, but the daughter is probably the one referred to in Granville's note to his mother. We have a birth certificate that shows the father as Smolenski, so you would think there would be a paper trail leading us to the daughter. Other than the birth certificate, there is no trace of this girl. It's like she dropped off the face of the earth."

Raising her hand to summon the waitress, Kate ordered another pot of tea and some toasted tea cakes. After the waitress left the table, Kate said, "I've been studying this man for over ten years now, and I'm very familiar with Smolenski's way of thinking. He wanted to be involved in her life if he allowed his name on the birth certificate. I bet he has recognized her as his daughter and made provisions for her but changed her identity to keep her safe from his enemies; believe me, he has many. If a rival gang got wind of a daughter, they would have no qualms of kidnapping her to pressure her father."

After the waitress brought their order, Sam asked, "Any ideas of how to track her?"

"I have a few. After we finish eating, I'll make some calls to some of my contacts and have them put out feelers, but I can warn you, Smolenski is a pro at keeping one step ahead of his enemies. That's the only way he has managed to stay alive all these years. Anyone who gets too close to him or anything he regards as his is a target for his assassins."

Sam looked up from buttering his tea cake, "You sound like you speak from personal experience."

"You're damn right. It's personal, so just shut up and eat so we can get back to the office," snapped Kate.

Sam dropped his half-eaten tea cake and went to the counter to pay the bill before walking to the door and holding it open, "Ready?"

No one spoke as they strolled back to the office. Kate felt bad about snapping at Sam and realized that the time had come to let him in on the reason for her early retirement. If they were going to have to go up against Smolenski, Kate didn't want to feel responsible for the death of another partner, especially one that, despite her actions, she was becoming very fond of.

As they approached the small park that bordered the office block, Kate asked, "Can we sit over there for a few minutes?"

A frown crossed Sam's face, "Are you feeling alright? Hey, listen, I'm sorry if I said something to upset you."

Sitting on a secluded bench, Kate patted the seat beside her, "Sit down. You need to know things about Smolenski and my past at the MET. I'm just telling you this for your protection and the protection of your team. My partner and I worked with a snitch who had always proven very reliable. I had gotten too close to some of Smolenski's assets, and rumors were that he intended to stop my meddling. A long story short, the snitch informed us that there would be a meeting at a certain address, and my partner and I were on a stakeout. It was an ambush. The assassins were pointing their weapons at me, ready to fire, then my partner knocked me out of the way before they could pull their triggers. I managed to kill one of them while the other fled the scene. My partner took all the bullets and died in my arms in that filthy alley."

"I'm sorry. It's never easy to lose a partner. Had the two of you worked long together?"

"Yeah, we worked and lived together for almost five years. Dan was my fiancé. The day I turned in my request to retire was meant to be our wedding day."

Sam didn't know what to say and suddenly felt guilty about his whining to Kate about being left at the altar, "Oh my God, Kate. I am so very sorry. I would never have asked Morgan to assign you to this case if I had known."

"Oddly enough, the connection with Smolenski was why he assigned me the case. The Commissioner is a wise man, and he knows me very well. Morgan knows I won't be able to move on until I get complete closure. Now that I have told you, I want your promise that you'll not tell anyone else. It's personal."

"You have my word."

The two detectives sat silently on the bench for the next twenty minutes before slowly strolling into the office, side-by-side.

Chapter 15

The autopsy report was lying on Sam's desk when he and Kate returned to his office. Briefly scanning it, he turned to Kate, "It's as I thought. Nicki has ruled it a suicide."

Knowing Sam was to brief Commander Morgan within the hour, Kate bit her lip, and her only acknowledgment was a shrug of her shoulders.

"Nothing to say," Kate?

"No, not at present. If you don't need me now, I have some favors to call in and see what we can dig up on Smolenski's mysterious daughter."

"That's fine. I will be on a telephone conference for the next hour or more."

Kate nodded as she gently closed the door behind her.

An hour later, a pale, sullen-looking Sam emerged from his office, walked over, and stood looking over Kate's shoulder as she searched for clues on the computer to the missing daughter.

"Can you take a break and step into my office for a few minutes?" asked Sam.

"Sure, what's up?"

Pointing at a chair, "Have a seat. This news might come as a surprise to you, or maybe not. I'm sure you know your soon-to-be former boss better than I do."

"Well, yes. I have worked for Commander Morgan since I started with the Force. He's an excellent officer and an all-around good man. I have the utmost respect for him."

"Well, when we discussed Granville's murder, I mentioned what his mother had told us. He suggested that we re-interview her. I told him about her suicide, and he started asking questions. I shared your opinions with him, and he not only agreed, but he is sending a team of pathologists down from London to review her death."

"Have you told Nicki?"

"Yes, I just phoned her before coming out to get you. I told her we respected her work, but those above us at the MET had made the decision."

"Oh my, what was her reaction?"

"Well, she went quiet for a moment and then said she had a fortnight holiday coming and was taking it effectively today. She asked me to pass on a message to you that she would probably be gone before you got home, so not to worry if you didn't see her for a couple of weeks."

"Oh damn. She is pissed!"

Sam sighed, "I think it's more a matter of hurt pride."

"Did she say anything else?'

"Yeah. Nicki said if anyone else ended up dead, the London professionals could damn well handle it themselves before she slammed the phone down in my ear."

Leaning back in her chair, Kate shook her head and muttered, Shit."

The afternoon drug on, but when it was finally time to drop Kate back at her cottage, Sam suggested stopping in for a meal at the Old Forge Inn close to Kate's.

"After the day we've had, I think a good fattening meal and a few pints are what the doctor ordered. My treat," replied Sam.

Kate selected the most isolated table, in case the conversation turned to Nicki, as Sam ordered the pints from the bar and picked up the menus.

Trying to lighten the mood, Sam smiled as he placed her pint in front of her, "Goodness, looks like you picked the most secluded, romantic table in the place."

Kate pulled a face before responding, "Actually, since the pub is so close to the cottages, I assume it's Nicki's local and probably her family's before hers."

Sam sat silently, looking at the menu, then suddenly looked up and asked, "What makes you think this could have been Nicki's family's pub?"

"Because she told me, when I looked at the cottage, how her grandfather had bought the cottage next door and extended it for his growing family."

Chuckling into his beer, Sam said, "That must be the story that she told all the holiday let renters."

"OK, what is so funny about that?"

"I told you that I spent the summers here with my aunt, right?"

"Yeah, so?"

"Well, her family didn't own or live in those cottages. Nicki bought it as a derelict and had it rebuilt. As a matter of fact, your cottage was previously a cowshed attached to the original cottage. My aunt used to take eggs and bread to the old gentleman who lived there. He was a confirmed bachelor and died at the ripe old age of ninety-seven, leaving no living relatives."

"That's so strange. Why would Nicki make up a story like that?"

Returning to stare down at his menu, Sam replied, "It really wouldn't be very good marketing to advertise the rental as a cowshed, now would it?"

"Oh, when you put it like that, I can understand why!"

Placing their order with their waitress, they settled back to relax and drink their pints before Sam asked, "Any luck on your searches for Smolenski's daughter?'

"Not a clue yet. Is there any news on possible prints on the murder weapon or from Eliza's house?

"Yes, to both, and that is one of the reasons why I suggested stopping off here so we could discuss in private away from the office."

Having raised her curiosity, Kate asked, "What can you tell me here that you didn't want to discuss in the office?"

Staring across the table at her, San continued, "There were no prints on the blade as we suspected, but you remember that wine glass we found sitting next to the bathtub?

"Yeah."

"Well, the prints on the stem were definitely Mrs. Roberts, but they managed to lift a partial from the middle of the glass. We ran a search of the database and found a perfect match."

"That's good. Where do we find this person, and when can we interview them?"

"That person is in this very pub, and I am interviewing her now."

"What? This is crazy!"

"It is until you remember that you accepted a glass of wine from Mrs. Roberts when we went to interview her. I suspect that either she filled a dirty glass with wine and took it to the bath with her, or someone with gloves grabbed it in the kitchen and placed it beside the tub."

"With everything going on, I had entirely forgotten that, but since you mentioned it, I remember looking back and seeing Eliza pour what was left in my glass into hers and drink it."

After the waitress brought them their Roast Beef dinners and wandered over to assist another customer, Sam asked, "What theory makes more sense to you?"

"I'm not sure yet, Sam. I can only tell you I didn't put that glass there."

Sam looked down at his watch before announcing, "Interview ended at 19:45, now let's eat before this gets cold!"

Chapter 16

Two days later, the London pathologists summoned Kate and Sam to the morgue, where they had finished a second autopsy on Eliza Roberts.

Upon entering the basement of the building, the first thing that Kate noticed was the cold and the smell. The second thing was the naked body of the victim lying exposed on the table. Kate wasn't sure what caused her to do it. It's not like she hadn't seen hundreds of naked bodies laid out on a slab, but under the harsh lights and the staring eyes, Kate felt compelled to cross the room and gently pull the white sheet over the older woman's remains.

Clearing her voice, she stepped away and introduced herself, "For those who don't recognize me from former cases, I am Detective Chief Inspector Kate Lambert. Detective Sam Adams is the lead detective representing the Devon Constabulary. What have you got from us?"

A tall, lanky lab-coated man holding a clipboard in his hands stepped forward, "What we have here is a clumsily attempt at disguising a murder as a suicide. To be quite frank, I'm surprised your coroner didn't pick up on it."

Sam stepped forward and replied, "In Ms. Hopwood's defense, she was in the middle of the tricky identification of Crown Prosecutor John-James Granville when this happened right on its heels. These were her first murder autopsies. As you might imagine, we don't get many murders down here."

"I understand that, and she did a commendable job identifying Granville so quickly; however, even a first-year student would have had difficulty missing all the apparent signs of foul play on Mrs. Roberts. By the way, where is Ms. Hopwood? We haven't seen her since arriving."

Kate quickly responded, "Nicki had already scheduled a fortnight's holiday. In all fairness, Commissioner Morgan didn't advise us of your work schedule in London or when we could expect you. We didn't think it was fair to ask her to miss her holiday under those circumstances."

"I understand. It would have been beneficial to have your coroner here, though."

Sam stepped forward to stand beside the body on the slab, "Perhaps now would be a good time for you to explain your findings."

Pulling the sheet back to expose the victim's face, the pathologist began, "It may not be too visible with the naked eye, but under lab tests, we could make out a handprint on the right side of the victim's cheek. From the print size, we estimate that whoever slapped the victim was female or possibly a man with very delicate hands, but that is extremely unlikely. Second, we examined the stomach lining and what your coroner claims were the stomach contents, and it seems our tests show some discrepancies."

Intently listening, Kate asked, "Discrepancies?"

"Yes, Chief Inspector. The stomach contents contained the remains of a pub lunch and a trace of white wine. The stomach lining shows quite heavy traces of wine but no food residue. It would appear that your victim hadn't eaten in the last 12 hours but had consumed a large quantity of wine. That leaves us wondering why. Is it possible that Ms. Hopwood mislabelled the specimen and the jar contained a different deceased stomach content?"

"It's possible. I'll need to check what other post-mortems were going on during that time frame," remarked Sam.

"The last thing that didn't alert her was the direction of the wrist slash marks. For instance, a person sitting in a bath will cut in one direction, while someone standing over the victim will cut in another. Now, don't get me wrong, even the most experienced may have missed this."

Kate backed away from the table, drawing the sheet back over, covering Mrs. Robert's face, "So you conclude that the victim was definitely murdered?"

"No question about it. The murderer assaulted her while the victim was either passed out or too drunk to resist. The murderer then removed her clothing, placed her in the tub, slashed her wrists, and disposed of the razor in the wastebasket. If you hadn't noticed that little mistake Chief Inspector, I doubt Morgan would have even called us in for this case."

Sam thanked the team of pathologists as he and Kate left the lab and climbed the steps out into the sunshine.

As they headed back towards the office, Sam asked, "What woman would have had a motive to kill Mrs. Roberts? I know she and her daughter-in-law argued the night before, but I can't imagine her as a murderer."

Kate started to giggle and put her hands to her eyes as Sam asked, "What's so funny now?"

Continuing to giggle, Kate exclaimed, "My God, man, you claim to be a detective. Don't you notice anything?"

"What?"

Trying to regain her composure, Kate replied, "I couldn't help but notice when Mrs. Granville handed us our teas that her hands were much larger than mine and slightly larger than yours. My best guess is Mrs. Robert's niece, who was involved with her son. Now we just need to find her, and so far, that hasn't been an easy task. Smolenski's daughter has managed to erase all clues to her real identity."

The following two weeks dragged by with no additional clues to the whereabouts of Smolenski's daughter. None of Kate's informers back in London had even heard a whisper regarding Smolenski having a child. It would seem that their investigation had run into a brick wall.

Chapter 17

Three weeks had passed, and Kate had no indication that Nicki had returned to her cottage. Knowing the young coroner's state of mind when she abruptly left on holiday, Kate was worried about her only close friend in Devon.

When Sam came to pick her up the following day, Kate invited him in for tea and expressed her concerns, "I'm really beginning to worry about Nicki. She's well past due coming back to work, and I've heard nothing from her. I owe her rent, which I usually just hand to her, but I can't just deposit it in her account without knowing her banking details."

Sam sat down at the table and picked up his mug of tea, "I haven't heard a word from her either, which is beginning to worry me, too. As for your rent payment, we may have her direct deposit details for her pay in personnel, and if so, they'll be able to help you with that."

"Does she always keep her side of the door locked between your two cottages?" asked Sam as he got up and turned Kate's key in the lock. The door swung open, and they found themselves staring into Nicki's kitchen.

"Guess not," replied Kate as she got up and walked through the door and into the cottage.

Looking around, Sam said, "It seems like she left in a hurry. Dishes in the sink and wastebasket not emptied. Is Nicki usually this messy?"

Shaking her head, Kate said, "No, she's a neat freak to the point of being OCD. I'm just going to check upstairs. You wait here."

Taking the stairs two at a time, she opened the door to Nicki's bedroom. Her eyes immediately went to the wardrobe. Nicki had utterly emptied it. All her clothes and personal items were gone, "Sam, can you come up here? There's something you need to see."

"Coming, Kate! Please don't tell me that Nicki's lying up there!" called Sam as he raced up the stairs.

"No, Calm down. Have a look around. I don't think Nicki is planning on returning anytime soon."

Shaking their heads, they went downstairs, where Sam emptied the rotting food from the refrigerator and took the full wastebasket out to the bin. "We better take care of this, or your cottage will start stinking soon."

After dumping the garbage, Sam returned the wastebasket and locked Kate's side of the cottage door before turning to her and saying, "until we know what is going on with Nicki, it might be wise to keep your door locked. If she has moved on, she may decide to rent it to strangers."

"Hopefully, we'll hear from her soon. Right now, I can only think about a strong cup of coffee and maybe a teacake. Grab your purse, and we can get on our way," said Sam.

As she got into the passenger seat, Kate mentioned that Nicki had promised to go car shopping with her, and she felt it was time to get her own vehicle.

"I don't suppose you have any spare time on Saturday, do you?"

Looking over at Kate, Sam said, "What? The Detective Chief Inspector isn't used to having a driver? Or is it just my company or my driving that bothers you?"

Punching him on the shoulder, "You know better than that. I would feel more comfortable having my own car if I need to go somewhere and you're not available. People will begin to talk if you always appear to be at my beck and call."

His eyes sparkling with mischief, Sam replied, "What makes you think that there aren't rumors circulating about us already? I must admit that I mentioned I had taken you to dinner a few times. I can't have everyone thinking I'm gay, now can I?"

"There is absolutely nothing wrong with being gay, Sam."

"What, you do think I'm gay, don't you? Nicki mentioned it once, but I thought she was just having me on."

"Actually, she was talking about why you didn't seem interested in any available ladies, and I said that perhaps you were gay. That was well before you told me about being left at the altar."

Dropping the subject, the two rode the rest of the way into town in compatible silence. Parking the car along the curb in front of the tea shop, they raced to the door as the rain came crashing down.

Soon as they had ordered and seated, the conversation quickly turned to Nicki. "You've known her longer than I have. What do you think is going through her mind?" asked Kate as she dropped some sugar cubes into her large coffee.

Stirring his coffee, Sam grew silent and thought for a moment and then said, "Either Nicki is humiliated and angry that her work has been questioned or."

117

"Or what?" asked Kate.

"Kate, did it ever cross your mind that Nicki is involved with this case somehow?"

Munching on her toasted tea cake, Kate replied, "I did ask her if she had ever met or knew anything about Mrs. Roberts, and she said no, but she didn't make eye contact with me and quickly changed the subject. But you can't fault the job she did identifying Granville as quickly as she did. If she were involved somehow, I think she would have delayed the identification or just disposed of the metal rod. No one would have been the wiser."

"Yeah, I suppose you're right. It's just that this disappearing act of hers has me jumping to conclusions."

Kate smiled and said, "Eat up, we better not be seen eating every meal together, or those scandalous rumors will really start flying again."

Jumping up from the table, Kate grabbed the bill and called back, "My treat," as Sam popped the last of his breakfast in his mouth.

When they left the tea shop, the rain had turned to a drizzle, so they left the car and walked the half block to the office.

Entering the building, Sam directed Kate to the personnel office on the top floor and hurried into the incident room.

"Any new leads today, team?"

"We've been reviewing the tapes from the day Granville disappeared but didn't pick up on anything new. The Detective Chief Inspector wanted to check them too, so we have set it up in the small office."

Bounding in through the door, Kate smiled a thank you and said, "Listen, team, you can drop the title. I'm just Kate unless you're introducing me to a suspect."

The team nodded and went quickly back to work. Leading Kate to the room set aside for her to review the tapes, Sam said, "I think you just made some new friends."

They spent an hour scrolling through the tapes until Kate froze a frame. "Have a look at this woman brown-haired woman in the mini shirt."

Sam muttered, "Nice legs."

Kate poked him in the ribs, "Not that, you fool. Look at her face. Who does she remind you of?"

"Can you enlarge it?"

Kate enlarged the shot, "If it weren't for the brown hair and facial mole, she would resemble Nicki slightly."

"Yeah, but if you look closely, I will almost bet money that she's wearing a wig, and the mole is just cosmetic," replied Kate as she brought her face close to the screen.

"Scroll forward and see if she interacts with Granville," replied Sam.

Scrolling forward, the young lady walked right past Granville without a glance and moved through the door into the next car.

"Well, no joy there. Based on our conversation earlier, maybe we just see things that aren't there."

While Sam talked, Kate continued to scroll until she reached the section when Granville left the train. Within minutes, the young lady in question exited the car in front and, after hesitating until Granville left the platform, headed in the same direction before veering off towards the woods and out of camera range.

Looking back over her shoulder at Sam, Kate asked, "What do you make of that?"

"Either they are taking the same shortcut, and she didn't want to walk through the woods with a strange man, or she is following him."

Nodding, Kate replied, "My bet is on the latter."

Chapter 18

Kate's mobile rang three days later, displaying Unknown as the caller. Knowing that her snitches often used throw-aways, she accepted the call.

"Kate, it's Nicki."

"Nicki, where are you, and when are you coming home? We've been worried half to death."

The silence on the other end of the phone spoke volumes to Kate as Nicki continued, "Not anytime soon, I'm afraid."

"Nicki, what's going on? Where are you? I'll come to meet you, and we can talk about whatever's troubling you."

"I'm afraid talking isn't going to help this time."

"Listen, Nicki, whatever is wrong. We can sort this out."

In the background, Kate heard the sound of a foghorn blaring as Nicki blurted out, "Have to go. I just wanted you to know that I'm still alive. It's been great to have a real friend I could talk to, even if for a short time."

"Nicki, Nicki! Don't hang up!" It was too late. Nicki Hopwood had ended the brief call.

It was Saturday morning, and Sam was due at her cottage to take her to the town's car dealers. Deep in thought, Kate didn't even hear Sam's car pull into the drive, and when he knocked on her door, she was still sitting in her robe.

Letting Sam in, he looked down at his watch, "Am I early?"

"No, have a seat."

Wrapping her robe tighter around herself, Kate entered the small kitchen and put the kettle on before dropping into the chair opposite Sam.

"I've just had a call from Nicki."

Leaning forward, Sam eagerly asked, "Where is she? Is she alright?"

"To answer your second question, she sounds extremely troubled, and as for her location, she refused to tell me."

"Can we track the phone number?"

"I seriously doubt it. Most likely, Nicki was using a throw-away. The only clue I have is that I heard the sound of a foghorn in the background before she abruptly ended the call."

"Considering the amount of coastline just here in the south, she could be virtually anywhere in the country, or on the Continent for that matter,"

The whistling kettle sound had Sam on his feet and into the kitchen as he took over the tea-making. Sitting a cup of tea in front of Kate, he said, "We know what day she left here, so I'll have the team check with the trains, airports, bus services, and ferries to see if she left the country."

Kate took her first sip of morning tea, "Better put an all-points bulletin out on her car while you're at it. Maybe, we can get a hint at what direction she went from the cameras."

Just as they were leaving the cottage, Sam received a call from the incident room.

"Adams, here."

"Chief, you better get over to Millstone Manor. Mrs. Granville was going through her husband's desk and found a note she thinks you need to see."

Turning the car around, Sam replied, "On our way."

One of the twins opened the door for them and immediately took them to his mother.

Pale-faced and shaken, she handed Sam the note.

Stay away from my daughter. Your handsome twin boys will pay the price if you hurt her.

"It's not signed, Detective. Who do you think sent it? Are my boys in danger?"

Sam handed Kate the note, who replied, "We are fairly sure we know who the sender is. To be brutally honest, Mrs. Granville, since your husband is dead and unable to interfere in this young woman's life any longer than I would say, there is no longer any need to worry about a threat to your boys."

Slouching backward in her chair, she said, "I told him that one day some girl's father or husband was going to come after him, and I was right. This is what got him murdered, isn't it?"

"Yes, ma'am. I'm afraid it might be. That is the line of investigation that we are following at this time. Your husband's death is an ongoing investigation, so I can't go into further detail now, but as soon as we possibly can, we'll share more information with you."

Sam turned back at the door and turned to Mrs. Granville, "I am aware that you believed something you either said or did may have caused your mother-in-law to take her own life. The autopsy confirmed this week that

Eliza did not commit suicide. There is nothing for you to feel guilty about."

Kate said, "I'm not sure that was much consolation," as they walked across the gravel drive.

"Isn't it worse to know a loved one was murdered than they took their own life?" she continued.

"That the person in question decided to end their life is easier on those left behind unless they believe they are the ones who drove the deceased to it," Sam retorted.

"I guess that's true," conceded Kate as she climbed back into the car to continue their drive to the car dealerships in town.

After viewing used compact cars in three separate dealers, Kate finally settled on a Mini. She had gotten used to riding in Nicki's and thought even she could manage the small car on the narrow Devon lanes. Sam nodded his approval as they left the lot, "I think you made a good choice. That's a nice little car. When can you pick it up?"

"The dealer said, in five days. Can you give me a ride back when I pick it up?"

"Of course! It's lunchtime. How about stopping off somewhere before I drop you at home?"

"Sure, but somewhere different for a change, if you don't mind. The pub is nice, but I'd like to check out some other local eateries."

Sam's face lit up as he smiled, "It's a beautiful day. How about a nice little place overlooking the sea that does some excellent fresh seafood?"

"Well, that sounds divine! My stomach is just grumbling, thinking about it."

The appropriately named Cliffside sat on a clifftop high above a small cove. The two detectives chose outside seating on the terrace to enjoy the sun's warmth and the gentle breezes and listen to the waves gently rolling onto shore.

Kate perused the extensive menu before finally asking, "Do you come here often?"

"It used to be a favorite when I was courting."

Kate put her hand to her mouth, trying to suppress the giggle that was about to erupt.

"What's so funny?" demanded Sam.

Laughing now, Kate said, "It was just your use of that old-fashioned word, 'courting.' Somehow, it just seemed funny coming out of your mouth."

Sam indignantly declared, "I do have a sensitive side. So, what were you going to ask me before your giggle attack?"

"I was only going to ask you to order for me. I'm sure you'll know what's best if you come here often."

As the waiter approached, Sam ordered two plaice dinners.

When their food arrived, Kate was amazed at the quality and portions. The fish covered her entire dinner plate, and three types of vegetables served family-style accompanied it. The chef had perfectly cooked everything, and Kate couldn't remember when she had enjoyed a meal more.

After finishing their main course, Sam asked, "Afters?"

Holding her stomach, Kate declared, "I don't think I could eat another drop!"

His eyes twinkling, Sam said, "Oh, come on. There's always room for Eaton Mess, as he signaled the waiter and placed the order."

After eating, they took a short walk along the cliff path with Sam pointing out local points of interest. Suddenly as they rounded a corner, Sam stopped and stared at a tiny cottage sitting farther up the hill.

Looking in the direction of his stare, Kate remarked, "What a charming little cottage, and just look at this view. There isn't much I wouldn't give to own that place. It looks like the owners are having some remodeling done on it. I hope they don't change it too much. It's perfect just the way it is."

"No, he's just modernizing and updating the inside, no changes to the actual structure.

Shading her eyes with her hands against the bright sunlight as she continued to stare at the rose-covered cottage, Kate asked, "Oh, do you know the owner?"

"You might say, intimately. I own Seaview Cottage. It belonged to my granny, and my mother inherited it. For reasons unknown to anyone in the family, she had bad memories of the house, and when her mother died, she just refused to step foot in it. I bought it from her last year. Would you like to see inside?"

"I'd love to," called Kate as she raced up the steep path towards the cottage.

The cottage inside was as picturesque as the outside, and Kate fell instantly in love with its classic features. Sam showed her his plans for the new kitchen and bath, including updating the plumbing and electrics. The downstairs consisted of a lovely kitchen diner with an open fire, a combination pantry/utility room, and a good-sized lounge with an inglenook fireplace, complete with a bread oven.

"Oh, Sam, this is just perfect," exclaimed Kate as she stared out the large window and looked down at the sparkling sea below.

"I'm glad you like it. I plan to remove that old window and replace it with a more energy-efficient larger bay window, with small side windows that I can open to smell the sea and hear the waves."

"Brilliant! I would love to see it again when you are finished."

"I'll make a note of that, Detective Chief Inspector Lambert. Now, would you like to see upstairs?"

The upstairs contained two small but cozy bedrooms and a large family bath. Sam eagerly pointed out where he planned to have a shower installed in addition to a soaking tub.

"Well, Detective Adams, I am duly impressed."

"Outside, there is an outbuilding and a wood store on the property that will need filling before moving in. Granny originally cooked over the open fire in the kitchen, but it'll just be for heat now on those cold, winter days."

"I'll look forward to seeing it when you are finished."

"Can I ask a favour, Kate?"

"Certainly, Sam."

"When it's time to buy new furniture and drapes and things, will you go with me and help me make the right choices to complement the house?"

"I'd love to, Sam. Just let me know when you are ready to go shopping. It's always much more fun spending someone else's hard-earned money than your own."

When Sam dropped Kate off at home, the sun was just beginning to disappear below the horizon.

"Thank you for a lovely day, Sam," said Kate as she leaned across the seat and placed a kiss on her partner's cheek.

Chapter 19

"What was I thinking, kissing him?" Kate asked herself as soon as she was alone in her cottage.

Walking around in circles in her small lounge, Kate continued the conversation that she was having with herself, "Don't be silly. I'm sure Sam just took it for a friendly kiss among friends to thank him for such a lovely meal."

Kate nodded her head in agreement to herself, but she wondered if she wasn't feeling just a little too fond of Detective Sam Adams.

If Kate had looked back at the car before shutting her door, she would have seen Sam with his hand on the cheek she had just kissed and the smile on his face.

After a quick shower, Kate was ready for bed and had just dozed off when her mobile rang.

"Kate, it's Nicki. I only have a second to talk. Please don't try to find me. I'm afraid that looking for me will put you in danger, and I have grown very fond of you. Please, for both our sakes, forget about me. I'm a lost cause. Got to go."

The call that woke Kate from her sleep was over so quickly that Kate wondered if she hadn't imagined it. Nothing could be accomplished by waking up Sam in the middle of the night. Her call to him could wait until morning. Falling asleep, it was Sam she dreamed of, not the missing Nicki.

The sun peeping through the curtains and onto her face woke Kate from her dreams. Padding down the stairs, she put the kettle on and popped some bread in the toaster. The toast was all she could manage after the big meal of the night before. As she enjoyed her breakfast, she thought about the cryptic call from Nicki the previous night. Kate was confident Nicki was somehow involved with the two deaths more than ever. She picked up the phone to call Sam.

Answering on the fourth ring, a sleepy-sounding Sam croaked, "Adams."

Kate said, "I'm sure of it now. Nicki is Igor Smolenski's daughter."

Wide awake now and listening intently, Sam asked, "What happened overnight to bring you to that conclusion? Never mind telling me now. I'll be to you in half-hour."

Quickly finishing her toast, Kate dashed upstairs for her shower, dressed, and sat quietly in her lounge when Sam tapped on her door.

Throwing the door open wide, Kate said, "Have a seat. Tea?"

"Oh yes, please."

Kate sat opposite Sam a few minutes later as he sipped his tea and watched her face.

"Ok, tell me why you think Nicki is Smolenski's daughter."

"She phoned again last night and warned me that searching for her would put me in danger and told me to forget about her because she was a lost cause."

Leaning forward in his chair, Sam asked, "Do you honestly think she killed Granville and his mother?"

"I didn't say that! I don't think she killed either of them, but I think she was the reason they were targeted. For

130

one thing, the note that Granville was sent clearly warns him to leave the writer's daughter alone, and we both believe that Smolenski sent that note. For the better part of thirty years, Smolenski has gone to extreme lengths to protect his daughter and keep her identity a secret. I think he is responsible for Mrs. Robert's death, too."

"Wait, why kill her? She was gone from his mistress' family well before he even met the mother of his child."

Shrugging her shoulders, Kate replied, "I don't know the answer to that yet. I guess we'll have to wait until I hear from Nicki again. If I ever do."

The two detectives sat silently in thought until Sam's mobile rang, "Adams."

"Ok, slow down. Where was the car found? Any sign of Nicki? OK, we're on our way. No need to call Kate. I'm with her now."

Kate was on her feet and grabbing her purse, "They've found Nicki's car? Where?"

"At the bottom of a cliff, it looks like someone deliberately pushed it over. There's a body inside."

Panicking, Kate asked, "Nicki?"

"No, not Nicki, a man. Emergency services are extracting his body now, so we need to move."

Arriving on the cliff top, Sam led Kate down the steep path to the isolated cove below. Tire tracks at the cliff top were a grim reminder that a car had gone over the edge onto the rocks below before landing on its roof in the sand below.

When Sam and Kate reached the bottom, one of the London pathologists sent down to review the death of

Granville's mother was waiting for them with a backpack over his arm.

"The victim has a single gunshot wound to the back of the head. SOCO found this bag in the car. It looks like close to fifty grand. Emergency Services were just loading the remains, sealed within a body bag, onto a stretcher. Reaching over to uncover the face, Sam looked at Kate, "Anyone you recognize?"

Turning her head to the side, she stared down at the haggard face, "He does look familiar, but I'd need to look through some mug shots of Smolenki's known associates to be certain."

Covering the deceased's face, Sam nodded to the emergency services that they could continue transporting the body to the morgue.

Sam said, holding the money bag, "Appears that we have found our hitman."

Shaking her head, Kate replied, "Either that or someone wants us to think we have,"

Looking out to sea, Sam asked, "But where's Nicki?"

Standing on the beach in this peaceful cove, Kate looked out at the vast expanse of water before asking Sam, "Would it be possible for a large boat to get close to shore here?"

Pointing out to the left, past an outcrop of rocks, he said, "Beyond that outcrop, the water gets very deep, and an ocean-going yacht could easily anchor there. Do you think that this is where Nicki was picked up?"

"I can't think of any other reason why her car was here. Can you? But who was this man, and why was he killed?"

Sam continued looking out to sea, "Might as well get back to the office. There isn't anything more we can do here. SOCO will go over the area with a fine-tooth comb to pick up any clues to what happened here."

After they climbed back up the cliff path to where Sam had left his car, he turned to Kate, "I'll bet you weren't expecting to encounter anything like this when you picked sleepy, rural Devon for retirement."

When they returned to the office, Kate booted up her computer to find that she had new mail. Nicki had emailed her.

Dear Kate: I want to let you know that I didn't murder anyone, but I did lie to you. I had met John's mother. It was quite by accident. I was sitting alone in the pub when I noticed this older woman staring at me. After a few minutes, she approached the table with the strangest look and called me Ellen. Then she seemed to regain her senses, apologized, and left. I called after her for some reason, "My mother's name was Ellen. People tell me that we look very similar."

She immediately turned to me with tears in her eyes and told me that she was my Aunt Eliza. I remembered my mother talking about her older sister, who the family drove away when she became pregnant. I invited her to join me, and we got talking. And I felt comfortable with her and shared some things about my private life that I shouldn't have. I told her about my relationship with a very influential man and that he was married. I had no idea until much later that she was John's mother.

I guess that you have discovered who my father is. I want you to know that I knew Eliza was a murder victim, and I disguised the autopsy to appear as a suicide. My father has gone to great lengths to keep my real identity

133

unknown, and when Eliza discovered that her son was my mystery man, she argued with John. John wouldn't listen to his mother or the threats from my father, and we all know how that played out. When John was murdered, Eliza went berserk and threatened to tell everyone my real identity. I called my father and told him that I would need to move again, and he told me to sit tight and that he would talk to Eliza. You know the results of that conversation.

You would have found my car and the body inside it by now. You can stop looking for the person who murdered John and his mother. My father doesn't like leaving anything to chance, so once his executioner had completed the contracts, he was silenced.

That's all I can say right now, except that I hope someday to be able to make up for all the trouble I have caused you. Thank you for being my friend. Until then,

Nicki

Kate was still staring at the email when Sam walked up behind her and peered over her shoulder.

"Oh, Sam, read this. It's from Nicki."

After reading it, he spun Kate around in her chair and placed his hands on her shoulders, "You were right about Nicki. I never could quite picture her as a cold-blooded murderer either, but she is still an accessory to murder, so we can't just forget her involvement."

Looking into Sam's eyes, Kate replied quietly, "The Nicki Hopwood we knew ceased to exist the moment she left the shores of Devon. She will have a brand new and untraceable identity by the time she reaches her next destination. Believe me. I know how Smolenski works."

Chapter 20

A week later, Kate received a phone call from a local attorney requesting that she call in at his offices. When asked what it was in reference to, he simply replied that it wasn't something he was at liberty to discuss over the telephone. Booking an appointment with the attorney, Kate went in search of Sam.

Finding Sam standing by the office coffee station, Kate asked, "What do you know about a lawyer named James Mallon?"

Sam took a sip of his coffee and headed back to his office, closely following Kate. "Why do you want to know? Are you planning on committing a crime soon?"

"No. Mallon just phoned me and asked that I come into his office, something urgent that he couldn't or wouldn't discuss over the telephone."

"Interesting. James Mallon is a highly respected and very expensive criminal defense attorney to answer your question. He has a small office here, but I understand most of his clients live elsewhere. He spends a lot of time in London defending felons."

"I see, but what could he possibly want with me? You don't suppose it has anything to do with Nicki, do you?"

"There's no way of telling until you go see him. Do you want me to come with you? I have met Mr. Mallon on numerous occasions."

"Ahh… wouldn't that look a little strange?"

"No, I'll just explain that I had to drive you because you haven't had time to get a car yet."

The appointment had been agreed upon for the following day. As Kate and Sam sat in the plush reception area, she tried to imagine what all the mystery was about. The buzzer on the receptionist's desk sounded, and she stood and opened the inner office door, "Mr. Mallon will see you now."

The inner office was even plusher than the reception area. As they entered the room, a tall, grey-haired man rose from his desk and pointed to the two chairs opposite his desk, "Won't you be seated? This won't take long at all. Can I offer you coffee or tea?"

Kate sat down and self-consciously smoothed her skirt beneath her, "None for me, thanks." The attorney looked over at Sam, Nodding, "I wasn't expecting you, Detective Adams, but it's always good to see one of Devon's finest. Now, shall we get on with business?"

With that, Mallon slid a set of keys across the desk to Kate and withdrew a document from a file on his desk.

"I have the deed to the cottage you are currently renting and the adjoining cottage here. You will find that the transfer of ownership requires your signature for completion,"

Kate's eyes grew wide as she pushed the keys back across the desk at him, "I can't accept that. Those cottages belong to Nicki Hopwood."

It was then that Sam spoke, "I'm afraid that Detective Chief Inspector Lambert is correct. As an officer of the law, Kate is prohibited from accepting anything that could be construed as a bribe, even if the intent was a gift. Nicki Lambert owned the cottages, and unfortunately, she is still wanted for questioning in an ongoing murder investigation."

"Detective Adams, I am well aware of the law when it comes to these matters, but it so happens that there is no question that the bequeath is above reproach since the previous owner is now deceased."

As she leaped to her feet, Kate stared open-mouthed, "Nicki's dead?"

"I have no idea, Ms. Lambert. I am speaking of the late Crown Prosecutor John-James Granville. It was John that bequeathed you the cottages."

Sitting back down, Kate looked at Sam and then stared in disbelief at Mallon, "I don't understand. I never met the man. My first encounter with him was finding his remains. I'm sure you know by now that Mr. Granville was kidnapped and murdered. When did he make this bequeath?"

Settling back in his chair, Mallon said, "I think now might be a good time for that tea, unless you would care for something stronger," he said as he pressed the buzzer on his desk.

"Tea will be fine," responded Sam.

As soon as the receptionist delivered the tea tray and Mallon had dutifully played mother, handing each of them a cup of tea, he began to explain, "John and I had known each other since law school, and we were very good friends. I will tell you that I never approved of John's lifestyle and often warned him that it would end in tears. A week before John was due to leave on his annual grouse shooting holiday, he stopped by the office and had me draw up these documents. John was involved with a young woman who he refused to give up. He even spoke of divorcing his wife for her. John shared that this young lady's father was, how shall I put it, 'connected,' but he hoped to convince him that he had her best interests at heart. He knew it could go either way. Unfortunately, it didn't go how he hoped, and we now know the outcome. The young woman never owned the cottages. They were always in John's name. He bought them and paid for all the renovations. She merely lived there rent-free."

Kate shook her head, "I still don't understand why he would have left the cottages to me. As I said, I've never met the man."

Reaching back in the folder, Mallon withdrew another envelope and slid it across the desk to Kate, "John left this for you in the event of his death. He sealed the envelope when he left it, so you are the first to read its contents."

Dear Ms. Lambert,

If you are reading this, I am no longer in this world. Please accept this bequeath as my debt of gratitude for your friendship with Nicki. By now, you undoubtedly realize that the poor girl has had a horrendous life. I had hoped to change that, believe me when I tell you that I loved Nicki very much, and I think she loved me.

If it is within your powers, I hope you will take pity on her and remain her friend. I am sure she is going to need one.

Sincerely,

John-James Granville

After reading the letter, Kate passed it to Sam and asked, "What shall I do?"

Before Sam could answer, Mallon said, "There is no legal or moral reason why you should feel it necessary to refuse the bequeath. If you feel uncomfortable living there, you can always sell it and donate the money to charity. The choice is entirely yours. I might add that the family has no knowledge of John's ownership of the cottages, nor will they ever, so there isn't any concern about claims from them. Take your time and let me know your decision next week."

Leaving the office and walking out into the bright sunshine, Kate looked to Sam for guidance, "I sure wasn't expecting that. Now, what do I do?"

"I know Mallon's reputation well enough that if he says there is no legal reason for you not to accept the cottages, then there is no question. What you need to decide is it the right thing for you, and only you can make that decision."

Kate replied, "When I was under the impression that Nicki owned them, and they were probably paid for, at least, partly by her father, I wanted nothing to do with it."

"Well, the letter from Granville certainly ruled that out, and he hasn't asked anything in return, except for you to be a friend to Nicki if she ever needs you. Which I'm sure you would be anyway. The Nicki we knew has probably taken on a new identity and is most likely sitting on some tropical island somewhere, soaking up the sun and drinking Margaritas. I doubt we'll ever hear from her again," Sam replied as she slapped Kate on the back and headed back to the office.

He couldn't be more wrong.

Chapter 21

Two weeks later, a telephone call from the authorities in Mauritius notified Sam that a body had been pulled from the sea off a private resort. The female victim was registered under the name Kate Lambert; however, a search of her lodgings produced a passport and suicide note signed by Nicki Hopwood and directing the authorities to notify Detective Sam Adams of the Devon Constabulary.

Slumping back in his chair, he prepared himself for the call he must now make to Kate. Picking up the phone, Sam started to dial and then abruptly hung up, grabbed his coat off the rack by his office door, and left the office. Driving to Kate's cottage, he tried to think of an easy way to break the news to Kate but decided that the direct approach was the best.

As he walked up the path to her front door, Kate flung open the door, "I had another email from Nicki, and I'm worried. I was just coming to see you."

Nodding and easing Kate back inside the cottage, Sam said, "You better sit down, Kate. I just received a call from the local authorities in Mauritius. It appears that Nicki walked into the sea early this morning and drowned. She registered under your name, but when the authorities searched her rental, they found her passport and a suicide note asking them to contact me."

Silent tears began to trickle down Kate's cheeks as she nodded, "I was afraid she would do something like that."

Sam asked, "Her next of kin needs to be notified, and her body claimed. Do you know how to contact her father?"

"Not personally, but I might know someone who can get word to him. I'm sure he knows where Nicki was staying and will be checking on her. There isn't an issue with him going to Mauritius to identify and claim the body since they don't extradite."

"I hadn't thought of that. Smolenski probably knows every move Nicki makes."

Kate said, "Nicki's death is one move that I don't think even Smolenski anticipated. He was so obsessed with keeping Nicki safe that I could almost feel sorry for him. The loss of his daughter will do more to harm him than the legal system ever could."

Getting up and leaving Kate sitting in her chair and staring off into space, Sam headed for the kitchen to make tea. Returning, he found Kate staring at the screen on her laptop, "Would you like to see the email from Nicki?"

Sam nodded as he handed Kate a cup of strong, sweet tea and moved to stand behind her chair to read the short email.

Dearest Kate,

By now, you would have heard from John's attorney about the cottages. I hope you will accept them. It would mean a lot to me to know that you are living there. I have been forced to move around so much that I have never really had a girlfriend with whom I could just be myself until I met you. I'm sorry that I had to keep so many secrets from you. I'm sure you understand now that you know who my father is.

I want to thank you for being my friend. I will never forget your kindness.

Sam sat in the chair opposite Kate and said, "I guess we can now close the file on the Granville murder investigation. With the contract murderer dead and now Nicki, there isn't anything else we can do. It looks like you can finally begin to relax and enjoy your retirement without me in your hair."

Kate leaned back in her chair and took a long sip of her tea before answering, "I'm not so sure. Things are just too tidy. There's no one left to lay this murder at Smolenski's door. I don't like it."

Tilting his head to the side, Sam asked, "I'm not thrilled about it either, but that's not what you mean. What are you getting at?"

"I don't believe Nicki walked into that sea."

"Are you saying that you think her own father had her murdered to protect his skin?'

"No, I'm saying the girl they pulled from the water isn't Nicki. I need to get to Mauritius before that body is claimed. I bet Nicki is alive and well; if she is, I'll hear from her again."

Before Kate could finish her sentence, Sam was on his phone.

"What are you doing?" asked Kate.

"Booking two flights to Mauritius, of course. We're partners, and I'm going with you."

The flight from Gatwick to Mauritius was a grueling 12 hours, and both Kate and Sam were knackered by the time they exited the airport. Once seated in their rental car, Kate asked, "Can we check into our hotel first? I really would like to freshen up and get some real food in me. I can't stand the food they serve on these flights."

Sam had noticed that Kate hadn't touched the meal provided by the airlines but had put it down to emotional stress brought on by the report of Nicki's suicide. "Of course, we can. I could use a shower and a fresh suit after sleeping in this one on the plane. I'm hungry, too."

After checking into the hotel, they arranged to meet in the hotel restaurant in an hour and went off to their rooms. When Sam arrived at the designated time, there was no sight of Kate. After waiting another half hour, he phoned her. A groggy-sounding Kate answered, "Hello?"

"Are you OK, Kate? I thought we were meeting in the restaurant in an hour."

"Oh god, Sam, I'm sorry. I just laid across the bed for a minute and must have dozed right off. Guess I was more tired than I thought. I'll be right down. Better order a pot of coffee. I think I'll need it."

Within fifteen minutes, Kate came rushing into the restaurant and dropped down in the chair opposite Sam; she apologized profusely, "I'm sorry to leave you sitting here alone like that. I know you must be starving."

Laughing, Sam said, "Don't apologize. Unlike you, I did eat on the plane. Then again, my mother said I would eat anything put in front of me. She used to call me her little human waste can."

Smiling now, Kate replied, "At least she didn't have to deal with a refrigerator full of leftovers."

Nodding, Sam agreed, "Yep, never any leftovers at our house."

Pouring her a cup of coffee, Sam asked, "Shall we go to the morgue right after we eat?"

Kate nodded, "Yes, might as well get that over with. That way, we'll know one way or the other whether Nicki is dead or not and if she is, whether she drowned herself or had help."

As soon as they finished eating and Sam had gotten directions to the morgue, they set out. It was a beautiful late afternoon, and Kate's head turned from side to side as she took in the views, "So, this is what paradise looks like," she mused.

"It is gorgeous, isn't it? I guess that's why so many people honeymoon here. Very romantic."

Nodding, Kate replied, "Yes, I can certainly see the attraction."

They had been driving for about fifteen minutes when Sam pulled to the curb beside the non-descript building housing the morgue, "We're here. Are you sure you're going to be alright?"

Kate turned to stare at Sam, "If I could provide the identification for my murdered fiancé, I'm sure I can manage this."

Turning away, Sam replied, "I'm sorry, I forgot."

Getting out of the car, Kate turned to him and said, "No, Sam, I'm sorry. My remark was uncalled for. You were just being considerate, and I was rude. Forgive me."

Reaching over and squeezing Kate's hand, Sam said, "No worries. Let's get this over with."

After showing the guards inside the door their identifications, they were taken to a room serving as the island morgue. The oh-so-familiar smell greeted them before they had reached the door.

Pushing the door open as they entered, a lab-coated man turned, "May I help you?"

Sam replied, holding up his identification card, "I believe we are expected. I spoke with Doctor Singh about the remains of an English woman allegedly drowned here."

Reaching out to shake Sam's hand, "I am Doctor Singh, and there is no alleged drowning."

Kate stepped forward, "Are you saying the victim didn't drown?"

"No, no, no. You misunderstand me. There is no alleged drowning. The young English lady did drown. She had water in her lungs. The classic sign of death by drowning."

Kate nodded, "I see. May we see the body?"

Shaking his head, Doctor Singh replied, "I'm afraid that won't be possible."

"What do you mean it's not possible? We have liaised with your superiors on the island and have received the necessary permissions to view the remains. We are investigating a double homicide and need to determine if this is an accidental death or another murder," responded Sam.

Shaking his head, Doctor Singh replied, "I am afraid again you misunderstand me. It will not be possible to view the body because she is no longer here."

"What do you mean she is no longer here? Where are the remains of Ms. Hopwood?"

"The young lady's death was ruled a suicide. A witness saw her walk into the sea, and her father testified that she had been despondent over the death of a loved one. I released her remains to her father just this morning."

Shaking his head, Sam looked at Kate and said, "He's always one step ahead of us, isn't he?"

"Yes, and there is only one way he could have known that we were coming to verify the dead girl's identity. Either we have a leak on our end or the government official here who cleared our visit is in Smolenski's pay."

"I agree, and I'll bet on the latter."

Kate nodded before adding, "And I'll bet Nicki Hopwood is still very much alive."

Sam said, "There's nothing more we can do here. We might as well head back to the hotel." They thanked Doctor Singh and left the morgue.

"By now, Smolenski's yacht has left port, so we might as well return home," replied Kate as she stormed out of the building, slamming the door behind her.

As they drove back to their hotel to pack for their flight, a tanned but weary-looking Nicki Hopwood leaned against the railing of her father's yacht and stared back at Mauritius. Watching as the weighted-down body of a young woman silently slipped over the side of the yacht into the sea, Nicki turned to the older man beside her and asked, "How many more people must die, father?" Flipping the ash from his cigar into the ocean, he put his hand on her shoulder before replying as he turned to walk away, "As many as it takes to keep you safe."

If he had only turned back, he would have seen a look in his daughter's eyes that no father would ever want to see. I was pure hatred.

Chapter 22

Two months had passed, and Kate was settling into her new home. She decided to remain on the side of the property she had grown accustomed to rather than moving into the bigger adjoining cottage while awaiting her retirement. It still bothered her that while on medical leave, the MET still had the option to recall her if needed.

That call came bright and early one Monday morning when her former boss phoned to inform her of an email he had just received.

"Good Morning Kate. How are things working out for you down south?"

"Just fine, sir. I was enjoying the peace and quiet of civilian life. I hope you're calling to tell me my retirement has finally gone through."

Taking a deep breath, Commander Morgan replied, "Not exactly. I phoned to tell you about an email that came across my desk this morning that I thought might interest you."

Crossing the room and dropping into the fireside chair, Kate said, "Go on."

"Well, it was anonymous, of course. But I think this might be related to your missing coroner. The writer states that Smolenski has withdrawn the contract on you. This admission of a contract points directly to his involvement in the ambush that took the life of your fiancée. Assuming this is true, who or what would make him do that?"

Running her hands through her hair, Kate stood up and began pacing the room, "Nicki, of course. We had grown very fond of each other in the short time we were acquainted. I think she is trying to keep me safe."

Morgan nodded at the other end of the line, "That was my first guess. We all know that Smolenski is a psychopath and doesn't have a conscience, but it appears his daughter has some influence over him."

"There was something else," continued Commander Morgan.

Still trying to absorb the information that Nicki was likely still alive, Kate asked, "What?"

"The sender mentions a young woman named Laura who apparently disappeared and was reported missing by her family two months ago while on holiday in Mauritius with an unknown man."

"You're thinking that this is the woman identified as Nicki?"

"Seems likely. I am having the unit check the missing person reports this morning, and as soon as I hear something, I'll get back to you."

"Thanks, sir."

"I'll pass this information on to Detective Adams, but I wanted you to be the first to know."

"I appreciate that, Sir. I see Sam later this morning, so I can fill him in if you like."

"Sam, is it now? But yes, that would be a great help. Things are hectic here at the moment with planning for the Queen's Jubilee security."

After hanging up the phone, Kate crossed the room to her small kitchen and put the kettle on for her morning tea. As the tea steeped, Kate knew Smolenski was responsible for the attempted hit on her, which killed her fiancée. Although Kate had assumed the ambush was carried out on the orders of Smolenski, this email was the first confirmation that he had taken out a contract on her. How could she retire now without bringing him to justice?

Kate was still mulling over her decision to retire when Commander Morgan emailed Kate a week later with the results of the missing person probe. As soon as Kate saw the attached photograph, she knew that this was the young woman who ended up on the coroner's slab, identified as Nicki Hopwood. The resemblance was uncanny. She would swear Nicki had a twin if she didn't know better. According to the report, the woman, identified as Laura Wrestler, was reported missing by her husband after not returning from what she had stated was a week-long trip with her girlfriends. When his wife failed to return, he contacted the friends involved, and they denied any plans to meet up that week. When her husband finally called the police to investigate, her seized laptop revealed emails from numerous men she had met for sex during the day while her husband worked. Upon searching the home, the police discovered that her passport was missing, and from there, it was a simple task to trace her movements. Laura Wrestler had boarded a flight to Mauritius two days before her body ended up in the morgue.

As Kate finished reading the email, she heard the crunch of tires on the gravel outside, announcing Sam's arrival. It was the weekend, and he had invited her to go with him to survey the work progress on his clifftop home, Seaview Cottage. Opening the door, she wasted no time telling him, "We have confirmation that Nicki is still alive, so the case is still open." Pointing Sam toward her open laptop, "I'll fix you a coffee while you read the email I just received from Commander Morgan."

After reading the email, Sam turned to Kate and asked, "So, does this mean you want to continue working on the case?"

Passing him the steaming cup of coffee, Kate replied, "Under the circumstances, I feel I have no other choice. The confirmation that Smolenski had ordered the hit on me that killed Dan has left me no choice. I have to see this case through to the end."

Sipping his coffee, Sam replied, "I guess another road trip is in order. We'll need to interview the deceased's husband and review her emails to see if we can discover who she flew off to Mauritius to meet."

Nodding as she paced around the small lounge, Kate replied, "The sooner, the better. I'll liaison with the home office and have them set up the appointment. Now, let's get out to that cottage of yours. I want to see how the work is coming along."

It was a beautiful sunny day as they drove to Sam's cottage. Arriving at the back of the house by the narrow Cliffside road, Kate climbed out of the car and stood silently watching the sun rays bounce off the waves as they came onto shore in the small cove below.

Sam's breath caught in his throat as he watched Kate, a smile on her lips, lighting up her face and the wind in her hair. To him, Kate was one of the most beautiful, natural beauties he had ever seen.

"It's just beautiful, isn't it? I could stand here all day and watch how the light reflects off the sea," said Kate as she turned to face Sam.

"You'll be able to be more comfortable doing that soon," smiled Sam as he replied.

"What?"

"I have a contractor coming out to install a two-car parking pad, and right, where you're standing, will be a terrace leading to the back door. It will be the perfect place to sit and have a cup of tea in the morning and watch the sunrise or end the day with a glass of wine. What do you think?"

"Sounds idyllic, Sam. It looks like you have thought of everything."

Rubbing his chin thoughtfully, Sam replied, "Not quite. You'll see when we get inside, and that's where you come in?"

Raising her eyebrows, Kate asked, "Me?"

"Yes, I'm holding you to that promise you made me the first time you were here."

Holding the door open for Kate, he ushered her into the cottage. "As you can see, the work is finished. I would offer you a cup of tea, but I don't have any cups, saucers, or even a kettle. Not to mention somewhere for you to sit to enjoy it."

Kate's smile grew wider and wider as she walked from one room to another in the cottage. "Oh, Sam, it's just perfect. You have done a wonderful job."

Sam nearly ran up the stairs with Kate on his heels, laughing at her enthusiasm. "Wait until you see the bathroom."

Seeing the beautiful white porcelain soaking tub, Kate immediately kicked off her shoes and climbed in, "This is even better than the one I have. It's deeper and curved perfectly to recline and have a good soak comfortably. You're going to love this, Sam!"

Laughing at her enthusiasm, Sam held his hand out to help Kate from the tub before replying, "I'll probably never use it. I'm more of a shower guy, to be perfectly honest."

Kate peeped into both bedrooms before staring back down the stairs.

"Did you bring a measuring tape and a pencil and paper? I'll need to take some measurements if you want me to help you pick out furniture. Are you planning on using curtains or some blinds?"

"Call me old-fashioned, but it's curtains for me. Except in the kitchen, there I was planning on an interior shutter. The window is too close to the cooker, and I wouldn't want to risk a fire."

Handing her the pencil and paper, he followed Kate through the cottage as she measured every window, asking as she went about color combinations that he had in mind.

"I suppose you're like most men and want a leather sofa for the lounge and a recliner of some sort."

"Actually, I don't. I prefer more soft fabrics. Probably a solid-colored sofa and an upright chair with an ottoman."

Smiling, Kate said, "I'm glad. That would be so much more in fitting with the cottage's style. I think that would be a wise choice. So when shall we go shopping?"

"Let's get this interview with the dead woman's husband out of the way first, and then we can arrange a date and time. It will give the contractors time to finish the drive in the back and make delivery easier."

"Good idea. I'll call headquarters and ask them to set the appointment when I get home, but in the meantime, I'm getting hungry and thirsty. Can we stop at the Cliffside before you drop me at home?"

"I was hoping you'd suggest that! I haven't done my weekly shop, and the cupboards at my flat are bare."

It was such a beautiful day that the parking lot was nearly full when Sam pulled into one of the last remaining parking spaces. The outside dining patio still had a few tables open as he directed Kate to a table overlooking the sea, "I'll get the drinks from the bar and the menus. What can I get you?"

"White wine would be nice, thank you."

Sam returned a few minutes later with Kate's wine and a shandy for himself.

Raising her glass to his, Kate toasted, "Here's to your beautiful cottage."

Clinking her glass, Sam smiled as he retorted, "And to me, having managed to get an interior decorator for free. Cheers!"

Staring at the menu, Kate responded, "Oh Sam, don't you know nothing in this life is free. I believe you'll be picking up the tab for all these lovely, expensive dinners that I will need to keep my strength up while doing all of your decorating."

"It will be my pleasure, Detective Chief Inspector Lambert of the MET. As long as you don't object to sharing them with a lowly country bumpkin detective from Devon," chuckled Sam as he raised his glass to hers.

Smiling and clinking glasses with Sam, Kate playfully punched him in the shoulder, "Country bumpkin,...now that's another phrase I haven't heard in a very long time. Where do you come up with these, anyway?"

Growing serious, Sam replied, "You may recall that I told you I spent a large part of my youth down here with my grandmother, and I'm sure I picked them up from her."

Thinking about how close she had been with her parents, Kat asked, "Didn't your parents mind you being away so much?"

"Not actually. There was only my mother after my parents divorced, and I think perhaps I reminded her too much of my father in appearance. She wasn't well pleased with him after he left her for his secretary, emptying the joint bank account."

"No, I don't suppose she was, but I can't see why she took it out on you. I'm really sorry to hear that," said Kate as she watched his face.

"In truth, she just wasn't very maternal. Granny, on the other hand, was the complete opposite. A more loving and kind person you'll never meet. You would never have guessed that they were mother and daughter. They were so different in every respect."

Just as Kate began to look at the menu, a waitress walked by, delivering two plates of fish and chips to the table behind theirs. Inhaling the fragrant smell as the couple doused their chips with vinegar, Kate threw down her menu and exclaimed, "It's fish and chips for me. That smells heavenly!"

Smiling, Sam replied as he waved his hand to attract the waitress and ordered, "Make it two fish and chips. That haddock smells delicious!"

Nodding, the waitress replied, "Fresh off the boat this morning, sir."

After the waitress left, Sam leaned across the table towards Kate, "Kate, I can't help but worry about you. What if that email is just a ploy to lull you into a false sense of security, and that contract on you is still open?"

"I tend to believe it's true, and I believe that Smolenski has done it under pressure from Nicki. I'm sure he's not her favorite person at the moment for killing her lover and aunt, and he'll do anything to keep in favor with his only child."

He nodded his agreement, "That makes sense, and I can just picture Nicki doing that. She was very fond of you, as am I."

Feeling a flush come over her face as she deflected Sam's last comment, Kate replied, "I feel very sorry for Nicki. She can't have had much of a life with him as a father."

As the waitress delivered their fish and chips, all talk of the case stopped as Sam and Kate dove into their meals. When they finished eating, Kate looked at Sam, "Thank you for a lovely day and a delicious meal. I can't wait to get started on your house."

Getting up to pay the bill, Sam replied, "It was a good day, and you're very welcome. We better move if we want to get that appointment set up with our newest murder victim's husband."

Few words were spoken on the drive back to Kate's cottage, each detective lost in their own thoughts. For Kate, her thoughts were back on the case, but for Sam, his thoughts were only on how much he was beginning to enjoy spending time with Kate. Warning alarms started to go off in his head.

Chapter 23

Two days later, Kate and Sam pulled up in front of the residence of Anthony Wrestler in Reading. Kate looked up just in time to see the front window curtains move. Within minutes, a tall, thin, balding man opened the door and stood waiting. It wasn't a particularly warm day, but the man she assumed was Mr. Wrestler repeatedly moped his brow.

"Looks to be on the nervous side. What do you think, Sam?"

"Yeah, let's get this over with," replied Sam as he opened the car door and started up the walk, followed closely by Kate.

Removing his warrant card, Sam introduced himself, "Detective Sam Adam. Pointing at Kate, this is Detective Chief Inspector Kate Lambert from the MET.

"Won't you come in? Excuse the mess. I find it hard to manage the three school-aged children, work, and keep up the house. I suppose I will have to hire a housekeeper, but god knows how I'll pay for that."

Kate's eyes scanned the room before replying, "Under the circumstances, Mr. Wrestler, you're doing an admiral job."

"Thank you. Can I get you something to drink? Coffee or Tea? I have both or perhaps something cold.

"Tea would be lovely," replied Kate trying to put the nervous man at ease.

When he returned with a tray laden with tea, sugar, and milk, Sam began by saying, "I know this is a tough time for you, but we need to establish what happened to your wife and who she met."

As Kate poured the tea, she gently asked, "Can you tell us about your wife? What was she like?"

Abruptly rising from the sofa, Mr. Wrestler walked across the lounge to the television and picked up a framed photograph before returning to his seat. He handed the photo to Kate, "This is my Laura. I took this photo on our last trip to the seashore. Lovely, isn't she?"

Turning the photo towards Sam, Kate replied, "Yes, she is lovely."

"My wife was much different than me, but they say opposites attract, don't they? She was what people call now an extrovert. She loved meeting new people, attending parties, and being very social. After settling the children for the night, I was happy to sit and read. Typical introvert, I suppose."

"What did Laura do to pass the time when you were home?"

"We took it in turns, putting the children to bed. On the nights when it was my turn, she spent her evenings on that bloody computer. The other officers took it when I reported her missing. That's when I found out what she was doing. I often asked her what she was doing; she always showed me recipes or home decorating ideas she had found on the Web. Like a fool, I believed her. You see, in fifteen years, she hadn't given me a reason to mistrust her. I don't mind telling you that it came as quite a shock."

As Sam took notes, Kate continued, "Did she often go on nights or weekends saying she was going with her girlfriends?"

"Yes, at least once every three months over the last two years, but after the first couple of trips, I never had cause to doubt that was what she was doing?"

"Why was that, Mr. Wrestler?"

"Her girlfriends would stop by the house a couple of weeks before the trip and sit around our kitchen table planning what they would do while they were away."

"Did you know these ladies?"

"Why yes, they worked with Laura before she stopped working to stay home with the children. Both of them were school teachers. Most of the trips revolved around historical places of interest."

"When your wife didn't come home from her last trip, and you spoke to these ladies, what did they say?"

Choking up with emotion, they told me that Laura had claimed to be going somewhere with me on the weekends they were arranging a trip."

"When did she start doing this?"

"According to her girlfriends, it started about six months ago. Now that I think of it, that's also about the same time that Laura began spending more and more time on the internet. I would come home from work, and the house would be messy, and no supper started. Laura was always house-proud and prided herself at having a healthy meal prepared when I came in the door."

"I see. Did you notice anything else? Had she changed her appearance in any way?"

"Now that you mention it, that's what caused our big row before she left for the last time. Laura had beautiful shoulder-length blond hair. I came home one day to find she had cut it all off. I couldn't believe it. She took great pride in her hair. I'm not saying she looked bad, just different, not like my Laura."

Sam nodded to Kate before asking Mr. Wrestler, "Could we see Laura's room?"

Standing, the widower said, "It's our room. Laura and I still shared a bed. The other police have searched it, but if you need to, come along. I'll show you the way."

"Following the grieving man up the stairs, Kate remarked, "You have a lovely home, Mr. Wrestler."

"Thank you. If you are interested, I plan on putting it on the market as soon as this is over. Too many memories here that a foolish error in judgment has ruined and cost me, my wife."

The room search yielded nothing that Kate and Sam weren't already aware of from the initial police report. After thanking Mr. Wrestler for his time, Kate and Sam returned to their car.

After buckling up and starting the car, Sam looked over at Kate and asked, "What do you think would cause a mother of three children to risk her life meeting virtual strangers?"

Shaking her head, "Kate replies, "I honestly don't know, Sam. Some psychiatrists claim it is all down to hormonal change. Frankly, I don't buy that. I think boredom, lack of attention in some cases, or just the feeling that life is passing them by and they are searching for adventure. Whatever it was with Laura, it led to her death."

As they drove away, Kate said, "While we're closer to London from here than in Devon, let's stop in and touch base with Commander Morgan."

Sam grunted his okay. He hated driving in London traffic and avoided it at all costs. Seeing the grim look on his face, Kate continued, "We can drive to Richmond, and leave the car at the multi-story and catch the fast train and be at Victoria in no time. When we return, there's a great Indian restaurant not far from the multi-story. My treat this time."

The mention of Indian food brought a smile to his face. Sam genuinely loved a good curry, and the hotter, the better, "You're on DCI Lambert. Richmond station, it is."

Chapter 24

Commander Morgan greeted Kate with a hug, then, blushing with embarrassment, turned and offered his hand to Sam. Apologizing for the obvious breach in protocol, Commander Morgan turned to Sam, "I've known this officer since the first day she joined the force. I have grown to treasure her and think of her as a daughter."

No one could have been more surprised by his confession than Kate. She knew her boss had always mentored her, but she had no idea he felt that way. Motioning for them to have a seat, Commander Morgan quickly changed his tone and became all business. Sliding two grainy photos across the desk, he explained, "Security cameras on the dock in Mauritius picked up these. You two know your missing coroner better than anyone other than her father, and I can't see him willing to help in this case."

Putting the photos side-by-side, the two detectives stared at the images. At first glance, it appeared to be Victor Smolenski welcoming the same blond woman aboard his yacht. Tilting her head from side to side, Kate asked, "Were you able to enlarge the faces?"

Reaching into the folder on his desk, Morgan slid two more photos across the desk, "It's the best the experts could do. Any better?"

Pointing at the photo, Kate looked at Sam, "The woman in this photo appears to have a small mole by her ear. Do you remember Nicki having one?"

Pushing his hair out of his eyes, Sam replied, "To be perfectly honest, Kate, I don't know. I never really looked at Nicki that closely."

"Sam, Can you get the office to fax up any photos they have on file of Nicki? While they're doing that, I'll try to reach Mr. Wrestler to see if his wife had a mole there," said Kate

While the two detectives made their phone calls, Commander Morgan watched with a slight smile on his face. Kate looked up from searching for the contact number for Wrestler but said nothing.

"The team is faxing them over now. Where's the fax machine?" said Sam rising from his seat.

Commander Morgan rose from his desk and, opening the door, gave Sam directions to the fax machine.

Getting no answer on the Wrestler's home phone, Kate looked across at her Commander, "What was that little smile for?"

"I was just thinking that you two seem to work well as a team now for someone who couldn't stand working with Adams barely a month ago."

Determined not to rise to his baiting, Kate began calling Wrestler's mobile number before replying, "He grows on you."

As Kate's phone call to Mr. Wrestler began to ring, Sam returned, shaking his head, "Unfortunately, none of our photos are from the right angle to see what we are looking for."

Kate held her finger up to silence Sam as Mr. Wrestler answered the phone, "Mr. Wrestler, DCI Kate Lambert here. Can you tell me if your wife had a small mole by her left ear?"

"My God, yes, she did. Have you found her body?"

"No. I'm afraid not. We have, however, found some security footage that appears to have been taken of your wife the day she landed in Mauritius."

After a sharp intake of breath, Wrestler asked, "May I see it?"

Shaking her head, Kate replied, "I'm afraid not. This photo could well implement the man in the photo with your wife's death and three other deaths which occurred in Devon. I am sorry."

"This man who she was with, do you recognize him?"

"I am sorry. This is an ongoing investigation, and I can't reveal any information about the other person in the photo with your wife."

"Well, that tells me you know who he is, DCI Lambert. All I can say is you better find him before I do."

"Mr. Wrestler, we are doing everything possible to bring the people responsible for your wife's death to justice. Please let us do our jobs."

After a few more moments attempting to calm down the bereaved widower, Kate repeated firmly, "Mr. Wrestler, you have three beautiful children. You're all that they have now. You need to worry about them and let us get on with our investigation. We'll be in touch as soon as we have any information we can share with you."

Hanging up the phone, Kate shook her head before turning to Commander Morgan, "All this has come as a terrible shock to him. He had no idea what his wife was doing."

Nodding as he leaned back in his chair, "Poor sod. I don't even want to imagine what he is going through now. So, we know that the man in the photo is Smolenski welcoming Laura Wrestler aboard his yacht, but that doesn't prove that he murdered her, and the autopsy showed she died by drowning. I had our people check with the resort where she stayed, and the security tapes have conveniently gone missing."

"Wait, Doctor Singh, the coroner, told us that someone on the beach testified that they had seen who we thought was Nicki walk into the sea and not return. Apparently, this man raised the alarm," said Kate.

"We're one step ahead of you there, Kate. We checked the report. Our witness was Mr. Smith, and his home address is 221b Baker Street, London."

"Well, we need to speak to Mr. Smith. Let's get out there," replied Kate as Sam started laughing.

"What the hell is so funny, Sam?" asked Kate glaring at him

"I'm sorry. I shouldn't be laughing," replied a contrite Sam.

"Kate, the address. Don't you recognize it? It's the fictional address of Sherlock Holmes," said Commander Morgan.

Kate began to feel the heat from the flush spreading from her neck to her cheeks, "Good grief, sorry! I should have recognized that address right away."

"Don't beat yourself up. The authorities in Mauritius didn't either, and they were so eager to rule the case a suicide so as not to ruin the tourist trade that they failed to ask the witness for a photo id," replied Morgan.

"Are you thinking that this so-called witness is the man who took Laura Wrestler for her last swim in the ocean?" asked Sam.

Nodding, Commander Morgan replied, "I will bet that the man Mrs. Wrestler met online was one of Smolenski's men. Maybe he showed her photo to Smolenski when he noticed how much she resembled Nicki, and from there, it was a short leap for Smolenski to contrive a way to make us think Nicki was dead and close the investigations."

"Sounds very plausible," replied Sam.

So, we are back to square one," grumbled Kate.

"Not quite. We have evidence that Smolenski at least had the victim aboard his yacht. We just need to tie this Mr. Smith to Smolenski," replied Morgan.

Shaking her head, Kate replied, "I've been following Smolenski for years. He doesn't leave loose ends. My best bet is that the man who Laura Wrestler went to meet is already dead and food for the fishes."

"Possibly. In the meantime, we just follow up on any new leads. Nicki has contacted you before, and I strongly feel that she'll reach out to you again."

Saying their goodbyes, Kate and Sam left the office and slowly made their way back to Victoria Station and their train back to Richmond.

Within an hour of leaving Commander Morgan, the two detectives were sitting down to a curry dinner at Kate's favorite Indian restaurant. The fragrant, delicious meal in front of Sam had his total attention, while it was apparent from the way Kate pushed the food around on her plate that her mind was on something other than her meal.

Sam looked across the table at a frowning Kate, "This is delicious. Thanks for suggesting it. Don't you like what you ordered?"

169

Suddenly looking up from her plate, Kate asked, "What?"

"From the way you are pushing your food around on your plate, I wondered if you didn't like it."

"Oh no. It's fine. I was just thinking about Nicki and wondering how she feels about her father now. I believe she was really in love with Granville, and I can't see her being happy about him being murdered in that fashion, especially with her father knowing that she would have to perform the autopsy on the man she loved."

Sam replied, "It seems like he was punishing her for refusing to obey him and break off the relationship."

"My thoughts precisely, and if I'm not very mistaken, I think Nicki is plotting her revenge. I'm sure she'll be in touch, and sooner than later.

Kate didn't have long to wait.

Chapter 25

They didn't notice her while she stood in the shadows of the parking garage. They didn't even see her when she walked into the Indian restaurant and sat four tables behind them. Nicki had disguised herself well. Ordering soup and water, she quickly finished her food and paid her bill. Giving the waiter a large tip, Nicki asked him to deliver the note she had carefully composed to the blond lady at the table with the dark-haired man before they paid their bill and left.

Leaving the restaurant, Nicki quickly disappeared into the crowd of city workers returning home from their day jobs as Kate and Sam signaled their waiter for the bill.

Bringing the bill, the young waiter handed Nicki the folded-up piece of paper and jokingly said, "The lady sitting behind you asked me to deliver this after she left. Perhaps you have an admirer."

Laughing as she took the note, Kate replied as she, pointed at Sam, "She probably wants to know if this gentleman is available."

Handing the waiter her credit card, Kate unfolded the paper and quickly scanned the note. Jumping up from the table, Kate demanded, "Which way did she go?" as she raced to the door. The astonished waiter shrugged his shoulders and replied, "Sorry, Miss, I wasn't looking."

Grabbing the discarded note from the table, Sam read it as Kate raced out onto the sidewalk, looking desperately for the sender. Turning his attention to the bemused waiter, Sam flashed his warrant card before asking, "Can you describe the woman who gave you this note?"

"Of course. The lady was very thin, not so tall with dark reddish hair, very fair skin with a mole here," he said as he motioned with his finger to just above his lip.

"What was she wearing?" asked Sam

"She wore a dark blue pantsuit, white top, and sunglasses."

When Sam had finished talking to the waiter, a breathless Kate returned, "I lost her in the crowd of commuters. No sign of her anywhere. For God's sake, Sam, I can't believe she was right here, and we didn't know it."

"I questioned the waiter, and Nicki was in disguise with red hair, a facial mole above the lip, wearing a dark blue pantsuit with a white top and sunglasses. I'm not surprised that we didn't recognize her, but I'm even more surprised that she would risk coming back to England so soon."

Leaning back in her chair, Kate read the note out loud to Sam,

Dear Kate,

I have been watching you and know you are on my father's trail. I hope all my anonymous emails have helped you move the case forward. I am very sorry that another woman had to lose her life in my father's misguided attempts to protect me. I had no hand in her death or the planning of it. I first knew of it when my father collected her lifeless body from the morgue, and I was forced to witness her body being dumped over the side. There is no need to look for the man she flew to Mauritius to meet. He, of course, worked for my father, and he drowned the woman, and you know how he repays his assassins.

I will continue to pass you as much information as possible in hopes that you can finally get your revenge. Yes, my father admitted to me that he was responsible for the death of your partner, just as he was responsible for the murder of the man I loved.

I hope you catch him soon, or I will be guilty of murder, and it will be that of my father. I don't think I can wait much longer.

Take care and say hello to that handsome, mysterious Detective Adams for me.

Love,

Nicki

"Well, Sam, what do you think?"

"I think Smolenski has much more to fear from his daughter than from the legal system. The worse we can do is put him away for a long time. I have a strong feeling that Nicki is planning something much more personal and painful."

"I think you're right. Smolenski has tried to control every aspect of her life, and she has reached her breaking point," replied Kate as she stood up and headed for the door, followed quickly by Sam.

Walking to the multi-story, Kate turned to Sam, "I'll bet Smolenski doesn't know Nicki is back in England."

"If he does, he will come looking for her," replied Sam."

"Yes, and that's precisely Nicki's plan. She's setting him up, Sam. If we don't find him first, she'll kill him."

The drive back to Devon was quiet as both detectives mentally tried to anticipate Nicki's next move. She managed to elude her father and make her escape

173

sometime after leaving Mauritius, but where had that journey taken her, and where was she now?

Kate was the first to speak just as Sam brought his car to a stop at Kate's cottage, "Nicki will somehow lure her father back to England. I don't know when or how, but I'm certain of it."

Staring across at Kate, Sam said, "I'm not so sure of that. Smolenski knows that coming back to England is too dangerous for him if he wants to stay a free man."

"Smolenski will risk anything for his daughter. He has proven that many times in the past. If he thinks that she's in danger, he will come."

"He never has before. He has always sent his men to do his dirty deeds and then conveniently eliminated them. I wonder how he explains their disappearance to the other members of his organization?"

"Simple, in the case of the murderer of Granville, the car went over the cliff after he lost control when the chasing police fired on the car, striking him in the head."

"Well, what about the one in Mauritius?" countered Sam.

"Again, very easy. Smolenski tells them that the murderer was paid well and sent to South America to lay low until things died down. After a while, he'll either be forgotten or rumored to have started a new life and stayed there."

Sam shook his head, "I can't believe that all of them are that stupid."

"Do you actually think any of them are brave enough to question him? Frankly, I don't," replied Kate as she climbed out of the car and headed for her cottage door.

Suddenly Sam was beside her and pulling Kate behind him.

"What the devil are you playing at, Sam?"

"Shhhh," whispered Sam.

"What?"

"Your security lights didn't come on," replied Sam.

Edging closer to the door, Sam pointed at the broken pane of glass, "Looks like someone's broken in. Stay behind me!"

Pushing her way past Sam, Kate entered her lounge and stood staring at her small dining table. A bottle of wine and a vase of fresh flowers stood in the middle of the table. A folded piece of paper was propped against the bottle of wine, identical to the one they had received at the restaurant just hours before.

"What does it say?" asked Sam.

Kate began to read the note out loud slowly.

I hope these flowers and wine will, in a small way, make up for upsetting your dinner tonight. Speak with you soon.

Nicki

Looking up at Sam, Kate groaned, "I didn't see this coming. I honestly didn't think she would be returning to Devon. She definitely has something planned. I just wish I knew what it was."

Less than ten miles away, a woman smiled as she stood on the balcony of her hotel room overlooking the Torquay harbor, "Yes, this will do nicely," she whispered to herself.

Chapter 26

He'd searched for her for two weeks since she left the yacht harbored in the small remote island while everyone slept. Finally, the message came.

Dad,

I just needed some time to myself for a while to try to put my life in order. After two weeks of trying, I now realize I need your help. I'm sure you know that I have returned home. I'm staying in Torquay. *If you anchor out, I can rent a boat and come to you. There are some things I'd rather discuss in private, so if your crew could be given shore leave, I'd appreciate it. I could fix your favorite dinner, just like when I was young, and things were much better between us. I want it to be like that again. Can we please meet?*

Your loving daughter

Smolenski smiled before turning and walking to the bridge to order the captain to chart his course for Torquay.

"We'll anchor well off-shore not to draw attention. My daughter will be joining me there. Now would be as good a time as any to give you and the crew a night of shore leave."

The Captain nodded, "The men will certainly appreciate that."

Humming to himself, Smolenski turned and headed for his private quarters to prepare for his daughter's visit.

Nicki was also busy preparing for the reunion with her father. She had gathered all the ingredients to prepare his favorite meal, but this time she had sourced a special ingredient for his salad.

It was still too early to harvest wild lettuce, but Nicki knew where to find it. She knew from all her years studying to be a coroner that ingesting too much of it would cause sweating, fast heartbeat, pupil dilation, dizziness, ringing in the ears, vision changes, sedation, breathing difficulty, and death. Knowing that her father always ate a large salad before his main meal, Nicki was sure of it having the desired reaction.

With everything prepared, Nicki rented a small motor boat from a concession at the harbor and made her way out past the yacht before circling back and boarding the vessel. Welcoming her aboard with a hug and kiss, Smolenski took her bags and led her into his private quarters.

"I hope you're hungry, Dad. I made your favorite salad and bought a steak that I can grill when you are ready," called Nicki from the galley.

As Smolenski poured them each a glass of wine, Nicki tossed the salad in her father's favorite dressing and placed the plate in front of him.

"I made it just the way you like it," said Nicki as she smiled down at her father before placing a kiss on the top of his head and settling in a chair opposite him.

"It looks wonderful. I'm so glad that you have come to your senses and returned to me," Smolenski replied as he began to eat.

"I hope you are enjoying your salad, father. I picked the lettuce just for you."

"What did you say?" he asked, wiping his brow.

"I said I picked the lettuce, especially for you. Can't you hear me?" Nicki asked sweetly.

178

"Yeah, you picked the lettuce," he repeated as the ringing in his ears grew louder and his breathing became labored.

Trying to stand, Smolenski fell back in his chair and looked glassy-eyed at his daughter, "I'm not feeling very good. Maybe you better call the captain and have him bring a doctor."

"Patting him on the arm, Nicki smiled as she replied, "Don't you remember, father, I am a doctor, and you are getting the appropriate treatment. You are getting just what you deserve."

Nicki returned to her chair opposite her father and patiently waited for him to become unconscious.

"Guess you won't be eating that steak, huh?" she asked as she put her fingers to his neck, checking for a pulse.

Walking to the suitcase she had brought when she boarded the yacht, Nicki removed two containers and began sprinkling the contents around the deck floor.

Without looking back, Nicki climbed down the ladder and boarded the motorboat she had arrived on. Motoring a safe distance from the yacht, she pulled an emergency flare gun from her purse and took careful aim at the vessel before disappearing into the night.

A loud explosion followed by the sound of sirens woke Sam as the Devon and Somerset Fire and Rescue Services battled to extinguish a fire on a superyacht anchored outside Torquay harbor.

By the time Sam arrived at the scene, the yacht had sunk. The 8,000 liters of fuel on the 85-foot superyacht led to evacuations from the marina and hampered divers

179

attempting to enter the waters to search for survivors or the remains of anyone who may have been aboard.

A few hundred feet away, a lone woman sat drinking champagne on her hotel room balcony overlooking the scene at the harbor below. Lifting her glass, she toasted, "Here's to you, Daddy. May you rot in Hell."

Epilogue

It was three days before the registration of the sunken yacht could be traced to one of the shadow companies belonging to Smolenski. Only one body was recovered from the sunken vessel, and identification was proving difficult. SOCO had easily determined that the yacht was deliberately set ablaze.

Kate had a strong feeling that somehow Nicki was responsible. Five mornings later, Kate's laptop binged, alerting her that she had mail. Taking a sip of her tea, Kate clicked on the mail icon and read:

Dear Kate,

I have attached a copy of my father's dental records. They should make it much easier to determine the identity of the man aboard the yacht, but let me assure you that it is my father.

I have set not only myself free but also you. We no longer have to be driven by the need to avenge our loved ones. I hope our paths will cross again someday, but in the meantime, know that I will always cherish our friendship.

Love, Nicki

p.s.

Why don't you give that lovely Detective Adams a chance? You two make a good team.

Nodding her head, Kate smiled as she whispered, "Maybe I will."

The End